AN ARCADIAN DEATH

BY THE SAME AUTHOR

DEATH TAKES TIME

MURDER CONFOUNDED

MURDER'S LONG MEMORY

A FATAL FLEECE

TOO CLEVER BY HALF

DEAD CLEVER

DEATH TRICK

RELATIVELY DANGEROUS

ALMOST MURDER

LAYERS OF DECEIT

THREE AND ONE MAKE FIVE

DEADLY PETARD

UNSEEMLY END

JUST DESERTS

MURDER BEGETS MURDER

TROUBLED DEATHS

TWO-FACED DEATH

MISTAKENLY IN MALLORCA

DEAD MAN'S BLUFF

A TRAITOR'S CRIME

A DEADLY MARRIAGE

DEATH IN THE COVERTS

DEAD AGAINST THE LAWYERS

AN EMBARRASSING DEATH

THE BENEFITS OF DEATH

EXHIBIT No. THIRTEEN

EVIDENCE OF THE ACCUSED

AN ARCADIAN DEATH

AN INSPECTOR ALVAREZ NOVEL

Roderic Jeffries

St. Martin's Press ❧ New York

Library of Congress Cataloging-in-Publication Data

Jeffries, Roderic.
    An Arcadian death / by Roderic Jeffries.
        p.   cm.
    ISBN 0-312-13922-5
    1. Alvarez, Enrique (Fictitious character)—Fiction.
2. Police—Spain—Mallorca—Fiction.   3. Mallorca
(Spain)—Fiction.   I. Title.
PR6060.E43A89   1996
823'.914—dc20   95-30039
                                                    CIP

First published in Great Britain by
HarperCollins*Publishers*

First U.S. Edition: January 1996
10   9   8   7   6   5   4   3   2   1

AN ARCADIAN DEATH

CHAPTER 1

Lavinia Grenville-Varney studied her reflection in the heart-shaped mirror set centrally on the elaborately inlaid dressing table. 'I wonder if the Hollands will be there?'

'Hopefully not.' Her husband was tall and straight-backed; his smartly trimmed hair was becomingly touched with grey; the small wrinkles about the corners of his eyes suggested long hours squinting into hot, colonial sunshine; his moustache was jaunty, but dignified; his manners were impeccable when not tinged with a sense of condescending superiority. Had he not in fact once been the colonel of a prestigious regiment, he would have been a fraud.

'I can't think why Serena invites them.'

'She's never sufficiently selective.'

She was silent for a moment, then said: 'I do wonder if her surname is Holland. Julia swears they're not married.'

'I shouldn't have thought he had the taste not to marry her.'

She studied her reflection with growing disapproval. 'These earrings don't go with the dress, which is a great pity.' She eased the ruby earrings free, replaced them with drop diamond ones. 'That's better . . . Where did he make all his money?'

'Some sort of trade.'

'Obviously. But what sort?'

'No idea. Not interested.'

She stood. 'The invitation is for eight, so we want to leave here at ten to and arrive at ten past.'

He consulted his gold Boucheron. 'That means there's time for a snifter.'

'I won't have one. Cedric always pours such strong drinks.'

They left the bedroom and went down to the large sitting-room from which there was a view of the sea to the south and the mountains to the west. He crossed to the cocktail cabinet. 'Are you sure you won't change your mind?'

'Quite sure. I've no desire to make a spectacle of myself by becoming thuffy, as Cecily's bound to do.'

'At least when she's half cut she forgets to try to imitate a lady.' He poured a whisky, added a splash of soda, lifted the lid of the ice bucket. 'Blast!'

'Pablo hasn't forgotten the ice again! They've both become impossibly slack. We'll have to sack them.' Then she spoke less certainly. 'The problem is, avoiding someone even slacker. Serena told me only yesterday that her couple are quite hopeless. I begin to think that all the locals are completely half-witted. I suppose it's due to inbreeding.'

'Wasn't much else to do before electricity and TV . . . I'll go and get some ice.'

'I hope they haven't forgotten to fill the ice trays.'

He left, to return within the minute. He put two cubes in his glass, crossed to one of the armchairs, sat.

'I tried to have a talk with Diana today,' she said.

'And?'

'Frankly, there are times when I just don't begin to understand our daughter. Her generation seems to take a positive delight in scorning standards.'

'Lack of any sense of duty.'

'I very tactfully suggested she saw more of Robert this time when he flies over to see his parents. Do you know what she said?'

'Could be anything.'

'School had put her off blancmange. She really can be quite absurd. Robert has a reasonable job; even if he is

6

only earning thirty-five thousand a year at the moment, he soon will be getting at least twice that when he's made a partner. And he's the only child, so he'll inherit everything. When I pointed all that out, she said I obviously agreed with that Quaäker feller. Have you any idea what she meant?'

'None at all.'

'Why is she being so unreasonable?'

'God knows!'

'She's beyond my understanding. What sort of future does she imagine Mason can offer her? When I asked her that, she claimed he's only doing the work until he's saved enough money to return home and finish his degree as a mature student. She said this showed he has unusual ambition and initiative.'

'He'll only have said that to impress her.'

'Precisely what I told her. Why can't she see the sheer impossibility? I mean, he's half Mallorquin. Can't she realize that miscegenation is totally contrary to nature? You must talk to her and make her understand.'

'Not certain that that's a very good idea.'

'Why ever not?'

'There's nothing fresh to say. My repeating it will only make her more irrational. That could run the risk of her leaving here and going to live with him.'

'She couldn't disgrace us to that extent!'

'Suppose we just let things take their course? My father used to say, A horse with bad breeding will never jump cleanly. One day he'll open her eyes to the impossibility of so unequal a relationship.'

As Tait descended the half-light of stairs, the volume of the music increased until it hammered at his ears. Most of the flats were let to holiday makers and it seemed to be an unshakeable rule that there would be at least one swarm of youngsters armed with what he believed was called a ghetto-blaster, played at full bore. As he reached the ground floor, opened the glass door, and stepped out into the cool of the evening, he longed for permanent release from this auditory purgatory. Yet softly, softly had to remain his watchword. Softly with the Ruig woman, softly with Mabel Owen. A skilled fisherman didn't try to haul in his catch as soon as it took the bait or he risked losing it; he played it until it could not resist being landed.

A short, paved path led him to the parking area, now in the shade of the block of flats. He unlocked his Renault 5 and settled behind the wheel. He was surprised when the engine started immediately and knew fresh optimism – perhaps it would keep going until he was able to buy a decent car.

He backed out of the parking bay, drove down to the main road, waited for passing traffic to clear, then drew across the road to head westwards. The sun had only just sunk behind the mountains so that their crests were starkly outlined. Some time before he'd been up at Mabel's house at a similar moment and he had remarked on the rugged mountain's brow robed in its azure hue. She'd treated his words with incomprehension. Into his mental file had gone the note not to wax poetical.

At the roundabout, he avoided a tourist Fiesta travelling

in the wrong direction – a fairly normal hazard – and bore right. Mabel considered herself to be a very smart woman, which meant she was vulnerable. Yet never to be under-estimated.

Her house, in an urbanizacíon which reached partially up the side of the hill, lay below the road and one's first impression was of a succession of roofs with no logical relationship. Few modern houses on the island did possess any sense of harmony. Yet however inharmonious its parts, the whole was worth a minimum of eighty million pesetas, even in the present depressed market. One could put up with a lot of discord when that sort of money was concerned.

He parked in front of the double garage. Her BMW was on the right, the servants' Peugeot 205 on the left. She was still far from convinced that since she owned only one car, it was reasonable to allow them to park theirs next to hers. In their ignorance, they might regard this as a suggestion of equality.

He descended the four stone steps to the front door, rang the bell, and as he waited thought about the day when he would have moved out of the flat into a home like this.

The panelled wooden door was opened. 'Good evening, señor,' Jacobo, dressed in black tie and white jacket, said in Spanish.

He suspected that behind Jacobo's welcome there was, as always, less than respect. But then it was, perhaps, difficult to respect anyone who paid court to Mabel.

Jacobo led the way into the sitting-room. 'Please to wait, señor.' He smiled, left.

Tait looked around the room, visually examining the furniture even though he could have described each piece from memory. He was no expert, yet was convinced that back in England the antiques would fetch at least a hun-dred thousand pounds. Surprisingly, although she had chosen for observable worth, she had also bought beauty.

He heard her singing as she approached. She claimed

that when young, von Karajan had heard her singing at a fund-raising dinner and had advised her to take professional training to ensure that she appeared at Covent Garden, La Scala, and the Metropolitan. Had that been true, it would have shown that von Karajan had a wicked sense of humour.

Accompanied by her snuffling Pekinese, she made the grand entrance on a tortured high C. Wrinkles half obscured by heavy make-up, she wore a dress that a woman half her age and girth might have managed without looking too absurd. He kissed her on the cheek since she claimed not to like full frontal. 'I'm late, my love. Humble apologies, but a spot of business cropped up just as I was getting ready to drive over. Forgive?' He bent down to pat the dog hullo since this was expected of him.

'Shall I?' For a moment it looked as if she might flutter her eyelids.

Most people considered her a stupid woman who lacked any sense of the ridiculous. But he could recognize the true person – a woman who preferred to be laughed at than ignored; who thought it ladylike to disclaim the slightest knowledge of finance, yet who watched over her assets with the eyes of a hawk; who had an instinctive good taste that was never quite overlaid by greed; who had a vindictive memory. A woman to be swindled with only the greatest care.

She crossed to a chair and sat, picked up the dog and placed it on her lap. 'Tell Jacobo to bring in the champers.'

A command more than a request. But he was careful, as always, not to show any resentment. He crossed to the small internal phone on the wall by the side of the bookcase that was filled with books for a cultivated mind – none of which, he was certain, she could have read – and pressed the call button. He passed on the command.

'I had drinks with the Tylers this morning,' she said.

He sat. 'Why the penance?'

Jacobo entered, carrying a silver salver on which were two flutes and a bottle of Veuve Clicquot in an insulated

10

container. He put the salver down on an occasional table, began to strip off the foil and wire cage.

'They served Rondel, not even a Codorníu. I think it must be true that they've been very hard hit by Lloyd's,' she said with satisfaction.

The cork popped loudly, catching their attention. They saw Jacobo spill a very little champagne before he could pour into a glass.

She said sharply: 'I've told you over and over again to be more careful.'

'It was very active,' Jacobo replied in his idea of English.

'He's utterly careless,' she complained to Tait. 'If I made him pay for what he wastes and smashes, he'd owe *me* at the end of the month.'

Jacobo handed each of them a glass, left.

She drank eagerly. 'Just because her parents have some sort of a title!'

It took him a moment to realize she was referring to Muriel Tyler.

'As if a title means anything at all in this day and age when even footballers and people like that get given them!'

To her, it would mean one hell of a lot. 'Bow, bow, ye lower middle classes!' He drank and as he listened to her decrying all those who assumed airs and graces, he decided that when the game was over and won, he'd drink only champagne, no more cava.

Her tone became coy. 'Bobby's trying to tell me something.'

'What a clever little boy!'

'He says my glass is empty.'

She used the dog anthropomorphically to point out things she thought it unladylike to do herself. At first he'd not realized this and had laughed because he'd thought she was being humorous; it had very nearly finished their relationship before it had begun to flower. 'An empty glass is like a politician's mind, it needs filling.' He stood.

'I'm not certain I should have any more.'

11

'Why not?'

'A girl has to be careful.'

When she'd been a girl, the widow Clicquot had still been alive. 'Just for once, live dangerously.'

'Bobby says you're wicked!'

He stood, refilled her glass and his own. As she drank, the Peke stared up at her, eyes bulging, snuffling loudly. 'Is everything going all right?' she asked, as she lowered the glass.

'As far as I can tell.'

'You make it sound as if something could be wrong?'

'The one thing I've learned from life is not to count the chickens before they're in the oven, never mind hatching. The Ruig woman is a very difficult character.'

'She's causing trouble?'

'Not directly, as I've already said. But I'm always ready for her to act illogically – illogically by our standards, that is.'

'When she stands to make a fortune?'

'A fortune in her terms.' He chuckled. 'But not in yours.'

'I should hope not . . . Are you saying that she can suddenly become very troublesome?'

'It's like this, my sweet. Because she's a peasant, one of her gods is money. But there is another, just as powerful.'

'What?'

'The land. There's a kind of primitive union some of them have with the soil. So until we have her signature on the contract, it's best to remember that she may suddenly renege because to sell will be to lose the land.'

'How could she be so stupid? . . . Should we offer her a little more to make her behave reasonably?'

'Now that might be a good idea! Concentrate her mind on money, not land . . . You're a genius!'

She simpered.

'So at the first sign of hesitation, I'll add another couple of million to our offer. Of course, that'll cut our take, but if it gets her signing . . .'

'I was thinking more in the region of a hundred thousand.'

The richer a person, the meaner. Still, that made sense since how did one become and remain rich without being mean? 'I think that if one is to snare her sense of avarice, the bait has to be sufficiently tempting.'

'But two million ... You don't think one would be enough?'

'Better not do something than do it by half.' He drank. Luck came to those who deserved to be lucky. He'd introduced the possibility of the deal's falling through not to persuade Mabel they'd have to pay more, but because in his opinion there really was the possibility that at the last moment the old woman would listen to her heart instead of her head. But now he could deduct most of that two million from Mabel's share of what she believed the profits were going to be. *Fortuna favet fortibus.*

CHAPTER 3

Mason tightened the last nut of the air filter, visually checked that everything was shipshape and Bristol fashion, went round the bonnet to the driver's side and climbed in behind the wheel. He switched on, turned the key. The engine fired immediately. He accelerated and the revs rose evenly. Satisfied, he switched off. As he stepped out of the car, the owner hurried over. 'It's ready?'

'It'll take you to Cathay if that's where you want to go,' Mason replied in fluent Spanish.

'Come and have a coñac before I drive home?'

'Thanks, but I'm meeting someone.'

'Another time, then.'

The man climbed into the Ibiza, backed out of the garage. Mason looked up at the electric clock on the wall and swore. Nearly an hour late. He wiped his hands on a rag as he crossed to the small, glass-enclosed office in which Vich was also working late. Fiddling the books probably. In Britain, a man who made an honest tax return was considered sensible; in Spain, a fool. He handed across a stained slip of paper. 'Those are the bits and pieces I drew from Stores. The hours are six and a half.'

'Taken you long enough.'

Those were the only words of thanks he'd ever get for all the extra work he'd put in. Vich was more concerned with profits than cementing good relations with his employees.

He left the office and changed out of his overalls. He hurried down the road to the front, impatiently threading a way through the drifting tourists. Would Diana for once have curbed her prideful impatience and still be at the Azul? Much more likely to have left the café over half an hour ago, angered by his neglect and determined to spend the evening with Richard. Richard Peregrine Cole. Precious enough to be in a museum of fine art. The only nephew of two extremely wealthy aunts, both of whom had left him their all. The boastful owner of a fifty-foot Riva, an Aston Martin, a house in Chelsea and another near Nice. And probably black sheets for an emperor sized bed in each property. With mirrors overhead . . .

He reached the front road and turned left. The Azul was the fourth café along and the outside tables of the intervening three blocked his view so that he still couldn't be certain whether, for once, she had waited . . . Then he saw her Titian hair. Richard Peregrine's riches hadn't done him a blind bit of good!

He came to a stop by the side of her table and when she looked up at him, he wondered if she experienced half the earth-moving wonder that he did when he looked at her. 'I'm sorry.'

'No call for an apology since obviously something much more important turned up,' she said indifferently.

When she was annoyed she began vaguely to resemble her mother; but even then it was obvious that her character was not cold, but warm and bubbly. He sat. 'I confess. A blonde in a topless Alfa wanted the nipples greased.'

'Is that supposed to be funny?'

'My humour's like last week's fish? . . . The job I started turned out to be a lot bigger than it looked.'

'And it didn't occur to you that since you were supposed to be meeting me at eight, you might finish it tomorrow?'

'The poor devil of an owner has been out of work for months. He's an appointment with a possible employer first thing tomorrow in Palma. If I hadn't fixed his car tonight, he wouldn't have been able to make the interview.'

'The good Samaritan!'

'A poor imitation of same.'

15

'That's true enough!' She smiled. 'In the circumstances, perhaps I should forgive you.'

He read all he needed to read in that smile and felt as if the sun had reversed its course and risen back above the horizon. A Mallorquin would have said, 'Love is like the seed of the datura, it strips a man of all reason.'

A waiter, sweat damping his face, came up to the table. 'You want?' he asked in English.

Mason looked across at the empty glass in front of Diana. 'What was in it?'

'Malibu.'

'And I'll have a gin and tonic, please.'

The waiter left.

'Dutch,' Diana said.

'Not this time . . .'

'Dutch.'

'I can't keep letting you . . .'

'I've told you, on the day you gain a first and are head-hunted for a job at the top, you're taking me to Paris and dinner at L'Archestrate and I'm going to order Canard Apicius.'

'What's wrong with Kentucky Fried in Charing Cross?'

'I really can't think why I bother with you.'

'Because you're looking forward to the dirty weekend.'

'I said nothing about staying in Paris after dinner.'

'Since when have you turned your back on a *digestif?'*

The waiter returned and put two glasses on the table, picked up the empty one in front of her, spiked the bill, hurried off.

Mason raised his glass. 'To a very long weekend.'

She did not respond and her expression had become almost bitter.

He studied her. 'Something's wrong?'

She looked out to sea. 'Earlier on, I had Mother at full bore.'

'The same old story?'

'Same story, different cast. This time it was Robert. His

16

parents live out here and he comes and visits them regularly; even they admit he's not dynamic.'

'Why's he so desirable in your mother's eyes?'

'The usual. The Dragon, Eton, Jesus.'

'You mean, he's a one-man revue? Breathes fire as he sings the Boating Song while walking on water?'

'You'd forget the third-form humour if you'd had to listen to Mother going on and on . . . Why can't she understand you're ten times the man Robert could ever be, even if he had a backbone transplant?'

'I'm flattered.' He would have liked to have felt as cheerful as he managed to sound. But how long would it be before her mother's poison seeds began to sprout?

CHAPTER 4

Very few Mallorquins knew or cared what was the origin of the expression, 'So stupid, he has more water on the brain than the knee.'

At the turn of the seventeenth century, five years before Don Quixote had begun to tilt at windmills, Mateo Vaquer, shepherding his father's small flock of brown sheep at the base of one of the mountains which ringed Canegot Valley, rounded a spur to come face to face with a woman dressed in white whose countenance spoke of unearthly suffering. His legs became too weak to support him and he sank to the ground. Within his mind, he heard the words: 'Be true, then truth shall flow for ever.' As the words came to an end, she disappeared and from the spot where her bare feet had stood there now gushed a fountain which reached a height of almost four metres.

Since it was the middle of the summer, Vaquer stared at the fountain for a long time, not daring to believe that his senses were playing him true; even the deepest well in the valley had long since dried up. But then a growing sensation of wet forced him to the conclusion that he was indeed lying in a flood of water which was surging over him to begin to spread out in the valley.

When he reached the huddle of stone buildings and shouted out the news, he was greeted with cries of addle-head, birdbrain, jobbernowl. But his mother called on everyone to witness the undoubted fact that his clothes were sopping wet and how could this have happened if he were not telling the truth? Men, women, and children, hurried from the village and when they arrived and found that he had indeed spoken the truth, they were awed and frightened. None of them, not even Jorge who was said to be ninety-two, had ever seen a jet of water, let alone one four metres high. To their simple minds, it was a miracle. They knelt and prayed.

But for events which had taken place in Tellitx, a few kilometres away, a miracle it would have remained. But twelve years previously, the daughter of a sot had been crossing a field when under an algarroba tree she had found a wooden statue of the Madonna. When she'd picked it up, the statue had spoken and told her that a chapel must be built in the field and the tree must be carved into an altar on which the statue was to be placed for all to worship. The girl had taken the statue home and related to her father what had happened. He had cursed her for an impious imagination that could send them all to the fires, grabbed the statue, flung it out of the house. As it had landed on the ground, it had disappeared with a clap of thunder. He'd transferred his curses to the seller of the last goatskin of wine he'd drained.

The next morning, he'd woken to discover that the statue was hovering in the air above him. Plagued by a thumping head, he'd made a grab for it, intending to throw it outside. His hand had been engulfed in flame, yet when he shouted with fear and dragged it free, his flesh was not even scorched. He'd immediately sought reassurance in a fresh goatskin of wine, but each mouthful turned to vinegar. The terror-stricken man renounced alcohol.

In the face of such momentous events, the church had conducted a thorough investigation. The exact nature of this had never been published, but as a result it had been decided by the bishop that a true miracle had occurred and the chapel should be built.

It proved to be an inspired decision. People travelled from all over the island – a few even from the Peninsula – to pray to the Madonna of Tellitx. For twelve years the faithful presented their offerings, many of which were silver, some of which were gold. Then, one Monday evening, as the scorching heat finally began to abate, news arrived that in Canegot Valley, Santa Margalida d'Antioquia (it had been the 20th of July) had appeared to a shepherd and caused a fountain to gush out of ground so poor and parched that nothing grew in it. Men cried that a second miracle had occurred and truly the island was a blessed land.

Those who served the Madonna of Tellitx were not convinced that the land had been blessed for a second time. After all, it could not be forgotten that since the number of pilgrims was finite, the value of their offerings must equally be finite and so if there were to be a second place of pilgrimage only a few kilometres away, each must benefit less than the one. Clearly, in order to make certain that the faithful were not being deceived, the claim of a second miracle must be rigorously examined.

The fountain proved to be an undoubted fact. Although no rain had fallen for nearly three months, it continued to spring into the air. The inquisitors turned to Vaquer and because he was so simple, they questioned him very closely. Their doubts proved to be justified. After a while, he admitted what had really happened. About to walk around the spur, there'd been a heavy rock fall and, frightened by this, it had been some time before he'd dared to discover what had happened. He had seen many fallen rocks and the fountain, but that was all. Certainly no barefoot woman clothed in white whose expression spoke of suffering beyond mortal ken.

Because there was the danger that there might be some who, despite Vaquer's recantation, sought a supernatural explanation for the fountain – perhaps by a mistaken analogy with the appearance of the Madonna of Tellitx – the two happenings were clearly distinguished. Only a miracle could explain the appearance of the Madonna. But it was known that below the surface of the island there were many pockets of water kept under pressure by overlying rock. In Canegot Valley, there had been one such pocket and this had been opened by a fall of rock and it was that which fuelled the fountain. A welcome bonus, but clearly no miracle.

Because those who lived in the valley lacked sufficient intelligence to accept as true whatever they were told was the truth, and because they were extraordinarily stubborn even for Mallorquins – had they not been, they would never have continued to try to wrest a living from the hitherto arid valley – they refused to be deprived of their miracle and, despite the official denial, continued to proclaim it as such.

There were many who demanded that these clods be condemned for their blasphemous stupidity. But those in charge were men of the world who understood that prosecution bred martyrs, laughter destroyed them. Let the men, women, and children of Canegot Valley claim what they would; it was, after all, God's will that they suffer as much water on the brain as on the knee . . .

The more they were laughed at for their stupidity, the more the inhabitants of the valley withdrew into a tight, isolated community and the greater became their belief. The fountain, which gushed through summer as well as winter, was much more than a column of life-providing water; it was an icon.

The water was, over the years, gathered into a huge estanque and from there directed through a network of channels to every part of the land. It turned the valley into one of the best farming areas on the island and the inhabitants became – in relative terms – rich, even though they were share-croppers and had to give half of all the produce to the owning family. When outsiders laughed at them now, it was more with jealousy than scorn.

Irony was a necessary part of every miracle. In the second half of the twentieth century, the introduction of mass tourism turned the economy of the island upside down. Scrubland which bordered the sea and would grow no crops and therefore had traditionally gone to the least favoured, work-shy son, suddenly became worth hundreds of times as much as the fertile land which had gone to the hard-working, favoured sons; a skilled farmer who laboured all hours earned less than a waiter.

The fountain of Canegot continued to flow as strongly as ever, but now it failed to provide the men and women with the privileged life of before. Some of the young began to leave, no longer content to remain in so limited a community, seeking the changed lifestyle that lay beyond the valley. Those who remained prayed to the fountain for the return of the past.

Beatriz Ruig, sitting under the shade of the century-old vine that trailed across the patio, supported on a rusty framework, heard the noise of a car. She squinted as she stared up the valley and halfway along it she saw a rising cloud of dust.

A woman hurried on to the patio. 'Doña Beatriz, there's a car coming!' she said, speaking Mallorquin with the thick, distinctive accent that inescapably marked her as coming from Canegot.

'Have you finished the work?'

'Not yet.'

'Then get back inside and finish it.'

She returned indoors. From time immemorial, women from the village had served the Ruigs for no wages; as the wives of share-croppers, that was their duty.

The car came close enough for Beatriz Ruig to identify it as Tait's decrepit Renault 5. Because she had not expected him, she experienced a sudden nervous worry that something had gone wrong with the negotiations. The thought of such a loss . . .

The car stopped and Tait climbed out. She didn't like him – there were none she did like – but she trusted him because he was English. Her father had taught her that while the English were arrogant, rude, and lacking all normal emotions, they were honest.

22

He walked up to where she sat, skirting some broken tiles just before he came to a halt. 'It's a hot day!'

What did he expect in June? He talked too much – in terrible Castilian – and he smiled too much. A person smiled when he wished to conceal his true feelings. Had he not been English, she would not have trusted him at all.

'I thought I'd drop in and let you know how things are progressing.'

'Well?'

'D'you mind if I sit?'

She didn't bother to answer.

He sat on the second rusty chair. 'You'll be very glad to hear things are going along smoothly. I should be along very soon with the contract to sign.'

'And the money?' She spoke Castilian so seldom that she had trouble pronouncing the odd word.

He smiled. 'I'm afraid I won't be bringing it in a suitcase! But the cheque should be through very quickly.'

'Twenty million?'

'You're getting the currencies mixed up again.' He laughed.

She flushed with anger.

'The deposit will be round about thirteen million, depending on the rate of exchange; less, of course, my expenses. By the time it's all over, you're going to be a very rich woman!'

From the day her father had died, she had saved the pesetas as avidly as he had once spent them. Every possible economy had been made. Her clothes had been darned to the point where little of the original material seemed to remain; she had eaten and drunk only what had been produced in the valley and therefore had cost her nothing; when the villagers had asked that electricity be brought in, she had refused because Gesa would have demanded a fortune for the work; when they'd claimed their houses needed repairs, she had pointed to her own which was in

23

a worse state of disrepair . . . Even so, the money had only grown slowly. Then she'd learned from an advertisement in a sheet of newspaper used to wrap up some eggs that her money could be doubled in a very short time. Had the advertiser been a Mallorquin, she would have treated his boast with suspicious scorn; but he was an Englishman and her father had told her that they were so honest that they could even be trusted with money . . .

Señor Sale had promised her that her four million pesetas would become eight in next to no time. Instead of which, it had become less, which had caused her many sleepless nights. But even she could face a loss if she was to receive a million dollars from another source.

CHAPTER 5

Dr Casanovas climbed out of his car and stared up at the house and wondered (with considerable annoyance, since he was a strong supporter of the move to preserve the island's past) how anyone could have allowed an old manor house to fall into such a state? Crumbling stone-work, missing tiles, rotting wood, damp . . .

A woman came through the arched front doorway, on the key stone of which had been carved a date that was now illegible. It was a long time since he had seen anyone so poorly dressed. She stood, her gaze averted. 'Well?' he asked.

'You are the doctor?'

He experienced only a brief flush of irritation at the stupidity of the question – he'd practised in Escalla for over ten years and had come to accept that the people of the valley had not changed with the times. 'That's right.'

He followed her into the house. The entrada was dark and gloomy and possessed a pervading smell of damp. The only furnishings were a damaged chair and a highly polished copper cauldron, set in the very large, open fire-place that had not been used for many years, in which grew an aspidistra. They climbed a narrow, stone-slabbed staircase, which had two quarter turns, to reach the sala, a large space once used to store produce and now empty and only dimly lit because the single, glassless window was small. At the far end were two doorways. The door of the one to the left had been smashed open and it now lay twisted about the lower hinge from which it had not been completely prised.

The bedroom was in near darkness because the solid wooden shutters – there were no inner glass windows – were closed. He asked her to open them. She crossed the tiled floor, lifted up the wooden locking-bar, opened the shutters to let in sharp light.

As he looked round the room, he wondered how Beatriz Ruig could have borne to live in conditions of such poverty? The matrimonial-sized bed, with barley-stick pillars at each corner, must once have been elegant, but wear and the years had reduced it to a state of shabbiness; the top sheet had been worn through and crudely darned and needed further repair; the lumpiness of that part of the mattress which was visible suggested it was filled with wool which had not been teased for a very long time. The rest of the furniture was in keeping. There was a large wardrobe, an ugly chest of drawers, and a dressing table, all of which looked as if they'd been left out in the open for a time before being brought into the bedroom; a chair with a broken back on which clothes were neatly folded; a wooden box some way from the bed on which was a metal candlestick with a protective glass funnel. On the ceiling was a large stain, caused by damp, that was edged with mould.

In the bed, the dead woman lay on her back, eyes closed, lined face only slightly contorted.

'Tell me what happened,' he said.

'We came to the house.'

'Because you were afraid she was ill?'

'Because we always come of a morning.'

Patience wearing a little thin, he asked: 'Why do you always come in the morning?'

'To do the cleaning.'

He realized something which he had noticed, but not consciously remarked. Despite the neglect and apparent poverty, the interior of the house was scrupulously clean. 'And when you arrived?'

'Doña Beatriz wasn't up.'

'That was unusual?'

26

'I said to Lucía, in thirty years Doña Beatriz has always been up to see we arrive on time. Perhaps she is not well. So we went up to here. I knocked. I called out, "Doña Beatriz, Doña Beatriz!" She did not answer.'

'You tried to enter?'

'The door was locked. We tried to look through the key-hole, but could see nothing. I said to Lucía, "She cannot be well." We did not know what to do.'

'But you did do something?'

'We returned to the village to speak with Frederico. He said we must enter her bedroom to find what was wrong. Pedro and him returned with us and they tried to open the door, but could not. So they looked for a heavy piece of wood and smashed the door down.'

'And you found her exactly like this?'

She nodded, crossed herself.

He pulled back the sheet, the dead woman's only covering. He was surprised to discover that she wore an elegant silk nightdress, most beautifully trimmed with lace. So she had not been totally bereft of a woman's vanity! An indication of sexual repression? He checked for rigor. It was present in face, jaw, and neck muscles, in the arms and trunk, and was beginning in the legs. The night had been very warm and the onset of rigor would possibly have been accelerated. Impossible to suggest a precise time of death, but probably between nine and twelve hours previously. She had gone to bed, fallen asleep, and died. Few were that lucky.

He gently rolled her over to complete his examination and saw the bruise on the back of her neck. Since it had not changed colour, it was reasonable to assume it had been suffered near or at the time of death.

He straightened up. The blow which had caused that bruise might or might not have been a contributory cause of death, but the surrounding circumstances seemed to rule out any suspicion of murder. Nevertheless, he was going to have to report the facts to the police.

*   *   *

27

Like many sparrow-small men, Inspector Garicano had a high opinion of himself and a low opinion of others. 'Well?' he snapped, as he stood in the centre of the sala and faced the left-hand bedroom with its shattered door.

Amelia stared at the tiled floor, her expression blank.

'For God's sake, woman, if you have a tongue in your head, use it . . . You found the door shut. Then what?'

'I knocked. I called out Doña Beatriz, Doña Beatriz!'

He'd not heard anything more absurd than to call the old hag who'd lived in the house, Doña. 'Go on.'

'We left to go to the village to tell Frederico.'

'You didn't try to open the door?'

'We couldn't. It was locked.'

'Then you did try. Didn't I begin by telling you that you must inform me of every single thing that happened? Didn't I?'

She nodded nervously, her gaze remaining on the floor, the fingers of her right hand fidgeting with her faded, darned cotton frock.

Only the last week, Garicano recalled, Superior Chief Salas had said that the Mallorquins were so stupid that even a Madrileño half-wit would find it impossible to have a conversation with them. He'd laughed a lot at that. 'Who's this Frederico?'

'He's . . . he's Frederico.'

'Does he live in the valley?'

'Yes.'

'What did he do?'

'He and Pedro smashed the door down.'

'And you all went inside?'

'Of course not,' she answered, shocked.

'Why not?'

'It was Doña Beatriz's bedroom.'

He must remember to tell Salas that; Salas enjoyed a good laugh at the ludicrous mores of the locals. 'So who *did* go inside?'

'Me and Lucía.'

'And you found she was dead?'

28

'We couldn't be certain. I mean, we thought she was, but . . .'

'So?'

'How . . . how d'you mean?'

'I mean, what happened next?'

'Frederico said someone must get the doctor.'

'Did anyone stay in the bedroom until the doctor arrived?'

She shook her head. 'We stayed out here.'

'Tell me exactly and precisely what happened when the doctor arrived.'

'He came in a car . . .'

'When you went back into the bedroom.'

'He told me to open the shutters.'

'Did you?'

'Yes. Only . . .'

'Only what?'

'That's not exactly right. He asked me, not told me.'

'A very subtle difference!' he sneered, not realizing the truth of his words. 'Were the shutters secured?'

'Yes.'

'How?'

'There's a piece of wood which slots into place to hold them.'

'Can they be opened from the outside?'

'I don't think so.'

'Were the inside windows open?'

'What . . . what inside windows?'

'The glass windows. You know what glass is?'

'But there's only the wooden shutters.'

No windows? In the last decade of the twentieth century! It was like entering the world of the troglodytes!

He went into the bedroom. He stared at the woman with distaste, looked round at the crude furniture with contempt, crossed to the window. The recess formed by the stone walls was roughly eighty centimetres thick. The shutters, on the inside, were made from thick wood and hardened by the years. When he swung them shut, the

29

crude hinges squealed. He picked up the wooden bar, some two centimetres square, and slotted it into the thick metal L-shaped brackets, initially having to use more force than expected. 'You had to lift this out before you could open the shutters?'

'That's right.'

He lifted the bar out, swung the shutters open. 'That's all I want from you at the moment.' As he watched her leave, he decided that she probably thought the world was flat.

The neatly folded clothes on the chair showed that until the dead woman had changed into her nightdress, nothing had occurred to disturb her. When she had changed, the door must have been locked and bolted and the shutters firmly secured. In other words, she had been on her own when she had fallen and suffered the blow to her neck – probably as she was about to get into bed. He looked around once more and quickly came to the conclusion that to suffer such a bruise without the flesh being torn, the only surface she was likely to have fallen on was one of the rounded tops of the barley-stick pillars at the corners of the bed. He visually examined them, including the two at the head which were almost hard up against the wall. There were no signs of contact, but that was hardly surprising because the wood was in such a state that further damage would have to be considerable before it was obvious.

As he had done from time immemorial, the old man turned the donkey cart left, ignoring the newly built roundabout which demanded he turn right. Inspector Garicano could not be expected to understand, far less accommodate, the local customs. He braked too violently on a surface disturbed by the heat and the car went into a dry skid and slid into a low wall. He had not bothered to fasten the seat belt and was thrown forwards and sideways. He was convinced he was dying, but the ambulance driver said he wasn't and the hospital told him he'd broken his nose, cracked three ribs, and suffered heavy bruising, and that was all. All? Only a half-educated Mallorquin doctor could have responded to critical injuries in so lighthearted a manner.

He would never curry his superior's approval because he was no sycophant, but to keep the superior chief clearly informed as to all that had been achieved in so short a time was a duty. A duty he would undertake as soon as he had recovered the strength.

CHAPTER 6

'Señor, it is Inspector Garicano speaking. I am having to talk to you from hospital because on the drive back from Canegot Valley I had the misfortune to encounter an imbecile in a donkey cart who left me no option but to endanger either him or myself; naturally, I did everything I could to avoid him. However, because I chose this course, I unfortunately crashed into a wall.'

'I trust you are not badly hurt?'

'The hospital refers to my injuries as serious, but I have always felt that a man's injuries are only as serious as he believes them to be.'

'An excellent attitude!'

'Naturally, I am ignoring the doctors' injunction not to bother about my work in order to report to you now.'

'Your sense of duty is admirable.'

'Thank you, señor. Dr Casanovas told me over the phone that he puts the time of death of Beatriz Ruig at between nine and midnight; of course, he added the usual proviso about these times only to be taken as approximate. He added that the bruise on the back of the neck was suffered very near to or at the time of death.

'One now has to consider whether she suffered an accident or was murdered; in either case, did this happen inside or outside the bedroom?

'Since she had a mobile phone over which she must surely have summoned help if attacked downstairs, we can rule out this possibility. She had changed into her nightdress and folded up her clothes and so we can go further and say that there could have been no attack up to this point. Before changing, she had locked and bolted the door and secured the shutters. I examined the shutters and can state without room for contradiction that they could not have been forced from the outside. Therefore, no one could have broken in and no one broke out. In other words, she could not have been attacked by anyone.

'Which means she suffered an accident. Once again, one has to ask, was it downstairs or in her bedroom? I questioned the doctor and it is his opinion that the blow to the neck would have left her groggy, but capable. If she had suffered it downstairs, would she not have called for help? Would she merely have gone upstairs, secured her bedroom, undressed, carefully folded up her clothes, and climbed into bed? ... Remembering the doctor's judgement that the bruise occurred at or very near the time of death, I suggest we can safely say that she was in her bedroom when she fell and on the point of getting into bed. Had she remembered to bring the phone upstairs, she might well have called for help; but she hadn't and perhaps not deeming the wound of much consequence, climbed into bed, expecting to be fully recovered by the morning. Instead, she died.'

'The doctor can't say to what extent the blow contributed to her death?'

'He won't hazard an opinion, but says the postmortem will have to answer that question.'

'Can he suggest what kind of object she fell on?'

'Not specifically. But because the skin was not broken, it must almost certainly have been round and possess a smooth surface.'

'Is there any suitable object in the bedroom?'

'The bed has barley-stick posts and these are topped with round, smooth wooden ball-like shapes. One of these would certainly inflict the kind of bruise she suffered.'

'I imagine you examined them closely?'

'Very closely. There are, however, no traces. But the wood is so affected by age and neglect that that is not really surprising. However, it does mean that we cannot prove that it was on one of them that she fell.'

'In view of all you've said, I don't see that that is of much consequence.'

'I would agree, señor.'

'Is that everything?'

'There is just one more thing. I intended to make a search of the rest of the house merely to confirm that there is no trace of the slightest consequence elsewhere. However, I discovered that almost all the rooms resemble overcrowded junk yards and the task would of necessity be a very long one. I decided to leave it for the moment and return when my other work was less pressing. Due to my accident, however, I shall not be able to do that for quite some time.'

'Have you any idea how long?'

'I cannot yet get a doctor to make a prognosis.'

'I'd like to see the case cleared up as soon as possible.'

'Naturally, señor. And it makes me feel guilty to be lying here, unable to . . .'

'Nonsense! . . . You are quite certain that the facts are straightforward?'

'I doubt that they could be more so.'

'There's not the slightest risk that a person of somewhat limited intelligence who possesses a delight in confusion might try to hold otherwise?'

'Impossible.'

'Then I'll detail Inspector . . .' At the last moment, Salas managed to prevent himself from naming names.

CHAPTER 7

Time was the servant of man, the master of a slave. Alvarez left the office early and arrived home to find Jaime seated at the table in the dining-room. Jaime pointed at the doorway into the kitchen and shook his head. The message was clear. Dolores was in one of her moods.

Women, Alvarez thought gloomily, were consistent only in their inconsistencies. 'Aren't you having a drink?'

Jaime pointed at the kitchen doorway again.

That he should so cravenly deny himself a drink! What had happened to Spanish manhood? Alvarez moved along to the sideboard, opened the right-hand door, and brought out a bottle of Soberano and only one glass. Then, noting Jaime's expression, he relented and reached for a second one. 'It's been one hell of a morning!' he said, as he sat after passing a filled glass across.

'You think it's been all fun for me. With her . . .'

He was cut short by a call from the kitchen. 'Is that you, Enrique?'

'Yes.'

Dolores appeared in the doorway. She looked the epitome of handsome, proud Spanish womanhood. 'I met Matilde in the baker's this morning.'

He wondered which Matilde she meant.

'She asked how you were and was very glad to hear you're well.'

'That's kind of her.'

'She has been a widow for a full year.'

'Poor woman.'

'Is that all you have to say?'

'What else can I say?'

'That you should need telling!' She spoke with long-suffering weariness. She stared at her husband. 'Is that your third or your fourth drink?'

Jaime, a man who seldom got his timing right, decided to assert himself. 'What's it matter if it's my tenth?'

'I will tell you exactly what it matters. I am not going to spend hours slaving in a furnace of a kitchen if the food I prepare is to be eaten by a man so besotted that he won't know or care if it's the slops for a tourist café.'

'It's my first drink.'

'And your last!' She put her hands on her hips, held her determined head high, stared at him with a challenge in her dark brown eyes.

If I want another drink, I'll bloody well have it, he shouted. But only in his mind.

She spoke to Alvarez once more. 'Matilde was saying that she's stayed on at the village house and not moved back to the finca because she'd be so lonely there.'

If she realized he'd no idea whom she was talking about, her ill humour would increase to the point where her cooking might suffer. He resorted to subterfuge. 'I'm never quite certain exactly where her village house is.'

'At the far end of Carrer Pa. The year before he died, Adolfo stripped off all the rendering so that the front is back to rock.'

He placed the house which finally enabled him to identify Matilde.

'It's a fine finca. There are ten hectares of good soil and two wells, the deeper of which never dries out. With a man to do the heavy work, it would once more be a very profitable property.'

The thrust of her conversation was suddenly clear – could any man want more than a widow with a village house and a desirable finca? 'That explains something.'

'What?'

'Why Estaban has been seeing her so often.'

'Estaban Bauza?'

36

'That's right.'

'She never so much as mentioned him. Who says he's friendly with her?'

'It's the talk.'

'Talk! You can find nothing better to do than listen to gossip?' She turned on her heels and disappeared back into the kitchen. A moment later, there was the sound of banging saucepans.

Jaime leaned across the table. 'Why are you so daft as to tell her something you must have known would annoy her?'

'Better be stung by a wasp than a hornet.'

'Hornet? She'll be a bloody tiger for the rest of the day.'

Alvarez drained his glass, refilled it. As Llompart had written, 'When a man marries, he loses first his freedom, then his friends, finally himself.'

He lay, eyes closed, recently awakened and still disembodied.

'Enrique. Are you up yet?'

He regretfully opened his eyes, gathered his courage, sat up, swivelled round, put his feet on the floor and, after further contemplation, stood and dressed.

He went downstairs and through to the kitchen, sat at the table.

Dolores said sharply: 'So now you expect to be waited on?'

'But you always . . .'

'Because I am a fool and have allowed myself to become no more than an unpaid servant in my own house.'

He hurriedly slid off the stool. 'If you tell me where things are . . .'

'And have you muddle everything up until I can find nothing?'

He returned to the stool. She cut a slice of coca, put this on a plate, banged the plate down in front of him. She made a mug of hot chocolate. The coca was light, the chocolate creamy rich. A woman who could cook divinely had to be forgiven much.

The phone rang and she hurried away to answer it. When she returned, she said: 'It's Palma, for you.'

He put the last piece of coca in his mouth, slid off the stool and walked through to the entrada which was kept even more spotlessly clean and tidy than the rest of the house because it was here that formal visitors were entertained. He lifted the receiver. 'Alvarez speaking.'

'I have been trying to phone you at your office,' said the superior chief's secretary in her unmistakable, arrogant, plummy voice.

'I've been down at the port, making inquiries. In fact, señorita, I've just called in here for some papers I need at the office.'

'I have a message for you from the superior chief. Last night, Beatriz Ruig died in her house in Canegot Valley. Do you know where that is?'

'Indeed. I can remember being taken to see the fountain by my father when I was very young. It was truly extraordinary!'

'Indeed.'

She probably had never been young and so could not begin to understand the bright colours of a childhood memory – the sense of utter astonishment at the sight of a thick column of rising water on an island where there were only torrentes and these ran only after heavy rain.

'The evidence clearly indicates that she suffered an accident in her bedroom. However, as is usual, a search must be made for negative evidence. You will conduct that search.'

'Señorita, Canegot Valley lies well outside my area.'

'The superior chief is quite aware of that. Unfortunately, Inspector Garicano has had the misfortune to be involved in a very serious road crash and he cannot conclude the investigation which he initiated.'

He'd met Garicano a couple of times. From the Peninsula and one of the new breed of detectives – academically clever, ambitious, self-satisfied.

'Do you understand your orders?'

'Regretfully, only up to a point, Señorita. I have to confess that I'm not quite certain what is meant by "negative evidence".'

'What else but evidence which proves a negative?'

'But what negative?'

'I am faxing full details. You are to study them and then proceed to Canegot Valley.' She rang off without bothering to say goodbye. As did so many secretaries, over the years she had adopted the style of her employer.

Alvarez dropped the last sheet of paper on to his desk, settled back in the chair, and stared through the unshuttered window. It was sad to learn that an old woman had died when completely alone. Yet had she not, in truth, been lucky? The knowledge of impending death must have been of brief duration, perhaps even absent. One minute light, the next darkness . . . He found it hard to believe in golden gates and singing choirs. Yet he found it even harder to accept that beyond lay nothing. Could man really have been called upon to struggle his way through life merely to meet the total extinction of death? One day he would learn the answers. But he didn't want to find out what they were.

He looked at his watch. Just after six. It would take roughly three-quarters of an hour to drive to Canegot Valley and so he couldn't begin work before it was time to stop and drive back. Thus he could find nothing, but it would not be the nothing he was ordered to find. He smiled at the absurdity of that before deciding that common sense clearly dictated he should wait until the morning before proceeding. It was a popular decision. He lit a cigarette . . .

The phone rang.

'Have you studied the case?' were Salas's words of greeting.

39

'I have just this moment finished doing so, señor.'

'Then understand this. Your job is solely to confirm that there are no suspicious traces anywhere in the house beyond the bedroom. You are not going there to question the evidence already ascertained. You are not going there to cast doubts on anything. Least of all are you going there to bring confusion to what is perfectly clear and straightforward.' The line went dead.

Would Salas have been less overbearing had he not been born in Madrid? Did the city make the man, or the man the city? It was an interesting question.

CHAPTER 8

Canegot Valley lay almost in the middle of the southern flank of the chain of mountains which ran the length of the island, forming a backbone. Originally only accessible by mule track, now it was approached by a lane which wound its way between fields of almond trees and then straightened up for the last five hundred metres to head for the mouth of the valley with arrow-like directness.

The mouth was no more than thirty metres wide and it held an air of foreboding because the walls of stone were almost sheer and on them grew nothing, not even a stray patch of weed grass. Through it ran a boulder-strewn torrente which came alive when there had been heavy rain in the mountains and because there was so extensive a catchment area, it could flow with dangerous force and speed.

Beyond the mouth – at which point the lane became a dirt track – the valley quickly widened and because the land was slightly higher it was possible to see to the far end. Alvarez braked the car to a halt and stared through the windscreen, fascinated by the contrast between the poor land through which he had just passed and the rich land at which he now looked. It needed no stretch of imagination to accept unreservedly that here grew the tastiest tomatoes, peppers, beans, peas, aubergines, cauli-flowers, cabbages, lettuces, sweet corn, potatoes, straw-berries, oranges, lemons, tangerines, plums, pears, figs, pomegranates, and grapes. Distant dots were cattle, sheep, and goats, no doubt each animal a study in perfection. He

41

drove on, along the very gently descending track, past a huddle of mean houses, casetas, and barns.

Three-quarters of the way along the valley, the land rose sufficiently to form a sugar-loaf hill and Son Abrut, a large, manorial house, stood in the centre of the top of this. At first impressed by its size, on close approach he was astonished to note all the signs of neglect. How could anyone have allowed so noble a property to fall into such disrepair?

He parked under the shade of an olive tree whose twisted, tortured trunk could truly have been a thousand years old. Once out of the car, he stared up at the tree's crop. When young, how many hours had he been forced to spend knocking green olives down with a long bamboo; and then how many hours – now with back aching as much as wrists – picking up the olives from the ground? Yet if he owned such a tree now, he would rejoice at aching back and wrists. He sighed. Some men were born to an estate; others could find one only by marrying a widow with a face like a turnip and a temper of fearsome proportions . . .

He walked across to the house, noticing the broken roof tiles, missing guttering, patches of damp, flaking plaster, and rotting woodwork. A proud owner would have had each repair carried out the moment it became necessary. It was strange how life so often decreed that those who were granted an estate by birth had not the wit to value it as they aged . . .

The heavy wooden front door, its surface grey and undulating because of the weathering of centuries, was open and he stepped into the entrada. For him, every old house had a soul and he was immediately certain that this one's was encased in ice. He called out and after a while heard footsteps to his right. He turned to face the low, arched entrance to the next room, above which turned the staircase. A woman came through, straightened up, stopped.

Her appearance astonished him. Her dress was clean and

recently ironed, but most women would have discarded it for rags; her shoes were square, clumsy, and to a pattern that almost all islanders had long since contemptuously rejected. 'I'm Inspector Alvarez, Cuerpo General de Policia. And you are?'

Her expression remained blank and she stared at the floor as she mumbled: 'Amelia.'

'It's beginning to look like it's going to be high summer right through to the end of August. Good for the crops, but not for working.'

She looked up, obviously surprised.

'I'm from Llueso and round there most of the shallow wells have dried up already, which is a month early. And down in the port they say that the water in all of 'em has become too salty for drinking. I was talking to a friend who works in a hotel and he says that's because the tourists waste so much water the sea's seeping in where the land's been emptied. They'll leave taps running in the bathrooms. You wouldn't have thought even foreigners could be that stupid, would you?'

His friendly manner was causing her puzzlement as well as surprise.

'I suppose you get tourists along here, looking at the fountain, turning the place into a rubbish dump?'

'Only one or two,' she replied.

'Count yourselves lucky! . . . By the way, I've come to look round the house – you don't mind, do you?'

'It ain't up to me.'

'I believe Inspector Garicano was here?'

'That's right.'

'And he didn't search anywhere but the señorita's bedroom?'

'He had a look in one or two of the others.'

'But didn't actually go into them?'

'Said he'd never seen such a mess. And that with Doña Beatriz not dead a day! She liked to collect things . . . What are you looking for?'

'Nothing specific. It's like this. It's certain the poor

señorita had the accident in her bedroom, but I have to make certain there's no sign of trouble anywhere else.'

'How can there be?'

'There can't. But I have to make sure there isn't.'

'Sounds daft.'

He smiled. 'I'll not argue with that.'

Despite the fact that it was a Saturday, he worked carefully. The interior of the house provided a strange contradiction. Every room but one – even the single, primitive bathroom – was filled with the confused junk of someone who could never throw anything away in case it might one day be of use. The exception was the study. In perfect condition, it was a window into past generations. On the marble mantelpiece were the knick-knacks of travellers who had wanted quality as well as memories and an elegant, antique clock in a domed glass case; the thick, velvet curtains, with gold-threaded draw-strings, were slightly faded, yet immaculately clean; the several matching chairs had seats in beautiful needlework; the two large Baluchi prayer rugs, rich with creams, whites, greys, russets, and blacks, filled one wall with elegance and mystery; the glass-fronted bookcase was filled with leatherbound books; the large desk had on it a silver pen and ink stand, a leather-backed square of blotting paper, a polished wooden notepaper holder, two silver-framed photographs, and a holder for pens and another for pencils – the silver was shining, the wood highly polished, the blotting paper unmarked; not far from the rugs hung a dozen framed photographs of men and women in the long, elegant clothes of the past and on another wall were hammer shotguns, muzzle loading rifles, bayonets, and a breast plate in which was a hole that might have been caused by a musket ball.

He left the study and went in search of Amelia, finding her in the kitchen where she was cleaning the highly detailed model of a pointer on point, in silver. The kitchen could hardly have been more wretchedly equipped, yet the tiled floor gleamed and the wooden table had recently been scrubbed.

'You've a job there,' he said, as he pointed at the silver dog.

'When it's cleaned every Saturday, it's not so bad.'

'You polish it every week?'

'Like all the silver in the grand room.' She put down the rag she had been using. 'I didn't know what to do, her being dead. But it seems right to carry on same as usual until someone says different.'

'Make sure you're paid!'

'That I won't be.'

'Why not?'

'Never have been.'

'The señorita didn't pay you for all your work?'

'It's me job; same as it is for me husband to give her half of all he grows. She owns everything.'

Share-cropping was a system that had largely disappeared throughout the island, but many years before it had been relatively common. Yet to have to hand over as much as fifty per cent of all the produce would have been regarded as very high, even when the workers lived in properties belonging to the landowner. 'With the crops you grow in this valley, she must have been a wealthy woman?'

'I suppose.'

'But you certainly wouldn't think so, looking around.'

'Many's the time I've said to my Miguel that half the work him and me do is wasted.'

'You'd have thought for a start she'd have kept the house repaired on the outside and in better condition inside.'

'We was told not to bother about anywhere but the grand room,' she said hurriedly.

'Why d'you think she kept that one room so well furnished and clean?'

'That's where she did business.'

He thought that there had probably been another and

stronger reason. 'Is it exactly how her father kept it?'

'All I can say is, it's been that way since I can remember.'

'He died a long time ago?'

'Before my time.'

'So you wouldn't know if they were close?'

'Who?'

'The señorita and her father.'

'Frederico says they was when she was young, but after her mother died things changed.'

'Who's Frederico?'

'The headman.'

That word was something else which irresistibly recalled the past. It held echoes of the time when most small communities had been isolated and largely ignored and authority had rested in one member, usually elderly because it had been believed that years lent wisdom and not, as now, growing imbecility. He began to see the anomalous state of the study as no more than a part of the much greater anomaly that was the valley. Those who lived in it inhabited a long-forgotten age. 'I'd like to have a look at her bedroom.'

Amelia led the way through to the entrada, up the stairs, and across the sala to the left-hand bedroom.

He studied the door, panels split and still lying as it had fallen and twisted. 'It must have taken something to smash *that* open!'

'They used a length of trunk that was going to be cut up for firewood this autumn.'

'Did she always lock herself in when she went to bed?'

'Can't say. Never been here that late.'

He thought for a moment, then said: 'Did you clean the bedroom regularly?'

'Me and Lucía did.'

'When you cleaned it, did she always stand and watch you?'

'That she did.' Her astonishment was obvious. 'How d'you know that?'

'Just a guess,' he replied untruthfully.

46

He stepped into the dimly lit bedroom, crossed to the window and, after a slight tussle, pulled the locking-bar free, opened the shutters and swung them back. One thing was clear, if the locking-bar had been in place – which it had – no one had come in by, or gone out through, the window . . .

The bedroom was not cold, but it chilled the soul if not the body. Voluntarily to have slept in a room so poorly furnished! And to do that when the study downstairs made it clear that she fully understood the meaning of comfort.

He pointed at the candlestick on the wooden box. 'Has the electricity been giving trouble?'

'What electricity?'

It was only after she'd said that and he'd looked for the usual fittings and failed to see any that he realized the house had no power supply. Which underlined his powers of detection! 'It's never been connected?'

'They wanted to bring it into the valley but she wouldn't pay.'

Was there another small community on the island that was without electricity? Had the cost been the sole reason for her refusal to have it or had she seen it as the Trojan horse that would destroy the time capsule in which the valley existed? . . . The extreme steps Beatriz Ruig had taken to secure the bedroom posed a further question. Why had she, in this time-warped valley, believed it so necessary to protect her honour; or had there been some even more precious possession to guard? The fact that when Amelia and Lucía had cleaned the bedroom, she had watched them all the time strongly suggested the latter answer. Her possession of a mobile phone was inexplicable unless there were reason for maintaining contact with the outside world which otherwise she shunned . . .

'Is there a safe or a strong-box in here?'

'Never seen none.'

He crossed to the large chest of drawers. The two half drawers and the next two full-size ones contained clothes which, although clean and ironed, one would not have offered to charity. The contents of the two bottom drawers added to the inconsistencies to be found in the house. Wrapped in layers of tissue paper were lace-edged, embroidered silk underclothes and night clothes in perfect condition. He looked up. 'Her trousseau?'

She nodded.

Sweet Mary! he thought sadly, but the tragedies of life were so often visible only to those who suffered them. When young, she would have made these clothes and as she plied the needle, dreamed of the Prince Charming who would ride into the valley to claim her. Only he'd never ridden and slowly her flesh had slackened and lined until one day she had looked in the mirror and seen a woman who never would be married. But because hope died only when imagination failed, she had occasionally, perhaps often, worn one of the nightdresses and in her dreams Prince Charming had swept her up and gripped her tightly about the waist as they galloped into the sunset . . .

'Is something wrong?' she asked.

He shook his head. 'Nothing.' The truthful answer would have been, everything. To understand another's pain was to discover one's own.

He crossed to the very large wardrobe, battered and heavily stained, and opened the two doors, both of which had lost the mirrors that had once been fixed to them. The smell inside was of old age and decay. The hanging clothes were little better than rags and some of the many shoes were virtually unwearable. Behind the shoes, in the far corner, was a strong-box, on the lid of which the letters G and R were still just visible. 'What was the señorita's father's Christian name?'

'Gaspar.'

He carried the strong-box over to the chest of drawers, set it down. Unsurprisingly, it was locked. 'Would you know where she kept the key?'

'Me? Not so much as ever seen that before.'

It was old and although it looked very secure, he was certain the lock was simple. Since he usually carried around with him a set of small lock picks – the kind of thing one never knew when one would need – he used these to force the lock. The fact that she had denied herself any quality of life made him certain the strong-box would contain a fortune in cash. In fact, there were ten five thousand peseta notes and a newspaper cutting . . . A man had only to congratulate himself on being really smart to discover he'd been talking to the moon. And yet facts remained facts . . . There had to be another hiding place. 'Where else did she keep very carefully locked up?'

'Nowhere.'

'There wasn't any other room in which she always kept watch over you?'

'No.'

'Even the study?'

'I've just said.'

Surely the dead woman would never have risked a second and far more important hiding place being found accidentally? So if this were not a secondary one, had she been a miser in poverty, not riches, hoarding junk because that was all there was to hoard? But when one remembered the crops the valley grew, it was impossible to believe that fifty thousand pesetas was all the wealth she had amassed in the years since her father had died . . .

He recounted the notes, signed a receipt which he dropped into the strong-box, put the money in his pocket. 'That'll be held by us until we know whose it is now.' He thanked her for her help, left.

CHAPTER 9

Sunday was inevitably shadowed by the thought that Monday followed. And, Alvarez thought gloomily, tomorrow he was going to have to write a report on his visit to Son Abrut, making certain his grammar was as good as he could manage because recently the superior chief had developed an absurd concern for the standard of literacy of all the work submitted to him . . .

'I want the other channel,' Isabel said shrilly.

'I'm going to watch my channel,' Juan retorted.

'Give me the control.'

'Shan't.'

A rough-house began, but stopped instantly when Dolores appeared in the doorway of the kitchen and said: 'Just what is going on?'

'He won't let me watch,' Isabel complained tearfully.

'All she wants is soppy stuff,' sneered Juan. 'In any case, it's my turn to choose.'

'It isn't.'

'This time,' said Dolores, 'I will make the choice. We will have silence.'

They were expert judges of their mother's moods and knew better than to argue when a certain tone was in her voice. After switching off the television, they left the dining-room.

Dolores stared at Alvarez. 'I suppose you were too busy to stop them fighting?'

'I was just about to . . .'

'Men! Always just about to, never actually doing. Unless

50

it's drinking. Without any regard for us poor, weak women.'

It seemed difficult to fit her into that category.

She disappeared as abruptly as she had appeared. He thought how pleasant it would be when he had retired and Monday was just like Sunday. Then he became aware that something was niggling his brain. Something to do with work; that had happened recently and might possess a significance he had not yet recognized . . . He drained his glass, refilled it, irritated that his mind could concern itself with work on a Sunday. He concentrated on a far more important matter. Did the smell now coming out of the kitchen presage Merluza Rellena? It was some time since she had last cooked that rich hake dish, with ham, garlic, egg, prawns . . . Dammit! His mind insisted on trying to identify whatever it was that was scratching at it. Something to do with Son Abrut? With electricity? But there was none . . . The candle in the candlestick! It had been only half burned which meant that it had been deliberately blown out since the glass funnel protected the flame from any draught. She would not have extinguished it before she got into bed. Once in bed, how did she strike her head? Alternatively, if she had initially fallen and hit her head on the post and, bewildered, climbed into bed, how could she have blown out the candle when it was roughly three metres away? . . .

Only fifty thousand in the strong-box? After years and years of miserly hoarding every peseta that came to hand? True, the returns to the farmer had gone down and down, thanks to the absurd agriculture policies, but she had not been bothered by rising wages and there could not have been any trouble in selling everything the valley produced. A not inconsiderable sum of money must constantly have passed through her hands, so where had it all ended up? . . . He was forgetting. The fifty thousand had not been the only contents of the strong-box. There had also been the newspaper cutting. It had not been large enough to act as a lining, so it must have had considerable significance for her. The side he'd briefly looked at had carried an advertisement for clothes and he'd assumed that she'd dreamed by day as well as by night. But now that he thought more carefully, he realized that the clothes had very obviously been designed for the young. However strong her dreams, could she really have seen herself dressed in the outrageous fashions of a modern teenager? Wasn't it very much more likely that the importance of that cutting lay on the other side which in his usual careless, unthinking way he had not bothered to read?

Lucía was working in Son Abrut and he introduced himself, though certain she must be able to guess who he was. Younger than Amelia and of sharper character, she was far more ready to express an opinion. 'I can tell you one thing, she was an old cow at times!'

'Was she mean?' Alvarez asked as he stood in the entrada.

'She wouldn't have given a loaf of bread to a starving child. Six months back I said to her that me and Benito was finding life difficult with prices like they are and so could she pay me and Amelia some money for working in the house? Know what she said? All the time we lived in her property, I'd do the work for nothing, like always. Benito spoke to a lawyer on the outside to ask if she could throw us out of the house when she wanted. All the time we don't pay rent, there's nothing to stop her.'

'You didn't think about leaving despite that?' he asked curiously. 'People aren't staying on the land as they used to, so you could find a good finca to rent. And there's work in the tourist hotels.'

'I suggested that. Tell the old bitch to find someone else to be an unpaid drudge. But my man was born in the valley whereas I wasn't; makes all the difference.' Her air of sharp independence gave way to one of worry. 'What's going to happen to us now?'

'All the decisions will have to be made by the new

owner, whoever that is. Amelia said the señorita had a cousin. Maybe he'll inherit.'

'He won't want to live here.'

'You've met him?'

'Been several times to visit the old woman. He's a foreigner. But he ain't.'

'What exactly does that mean?'

'His mother married an Englishman and he's lived in England until recently. Speaks Castilian as good as you and me. Not much Mallorquin, though.'

'One thing's for sure. If he is the heir and has more common sense than his aunt, he'll do something about the buildings. Always provided, of course, that there's the money.'

'She must have left a fortune, seeing what she's taken from the likes of us and not spent any of it.'

'We'll know one way or the other quite soon.' He crossed to the stairs and climbed them. He was not surprised when she followed.

In the bedroom, he brought the strong-box out of the wardrobe, set it on the chest of drawers.

'Amelia said about this. Never knew it was there. Is that where she kept all her money?'

'Didn't Amelia say it only had fifty thousand in it?'

'I thought she must be wrong.'

'D'you think that could have been her entire fortune?'

Her laugh was ugly, not joyful. 'If that's all she had, she must have been eating the stuff.'

He opened the strong-box and brought out the cutting. On the second side was another advertisement. In bold type, the question was asked: 'Do you want to be rich?' In smaller type, there was a second question: 'Do you want a large return on your capital AND strong capital appreciation that will double your money?' Did anyone not yearn for such miracles? he wondered. He read on. Profitable investment demanded expert knowledge. Throughout his working life, the author had been a partner in one of the most prestigious investment firms in the

City of London; he had handled the portfolios of the rich and of the not so rich; in every case, the clients' needs and the defence of capital had dictated investment strategy ... 'This wonderful Island of Calm has granted me so many happy moments and so much warm friendship that I should like to repay a little of what I have received. I have therefore decided to forego my retirement to the extent of helping a selected few investors realize their dreams. If you have capital to invest, if you wish to earn up to twenty per cent interest, and if in addition you welcome seeing your capital double in next to no time, phone me and we will discuss the possibility of my handling your investments.'

Could anyone be so naïve as to be taken in by this absurd offer? was his immediate response. Then he answered his own question. If Beatriz Ruig had been, there was the explanation for the lack of money in the strong-box. And when one thought about it, what could more appeal to a miser than watching her money earn high interest and increase? And since money had possessed her soul, would she not have needed to watch it earn and grow and what better way of doing that than to be in constant touch with the magician who could reassure her that his wand was working? Which would explain the mobile telephone ... Accept Leslie Sale as the conman his advertisement suggested. So contemptuous of the intelligence of the people he intended to swindle that he offered them the stars as well as the moon. Might not that contempt have led him to become so careless that she had discovered she had been swindled? The loss of her money would have enraged her beyond measure. She would have sworn to expose him ...

Alvarez pocketed the cutting, closed the strong-box, returned it to the wardrobe. 'Where will I find Frederico?'

'Out in the fields.'

He returned to his car.

CHAPTER 10

On his previous visit to the valley, he had been in a hurry, this time he was not. He switched off the engine, left the car, and walked alongside a major irrigation channel to the fountain.

Soon after it had appeared, the villagers had ringed its mouth with a circle of stone, carved with scenes that were intended to express their wondering gratitude. Over the centuries, the circle had had to be renewed more than once because of the constant weathering from damp and each time the original scenes had been reproduced as exactly as possible. Whoever had been the last artist had had more faith than skill.

The fountain arched down to fill a huge estanque with a sound hardly ever heard anywhere else on the island. He was hazy about the story, beyond the fact that at the time of its appearance, many had regarded it as a miracle. It was, provided one forewent modern cynicism, easy to understand and even in a sense to share this belief. Mallorca was an island which had always been blessed with water beyond the rain which fell on it, but in the height of the summer only the deepest of the wells did not dry up – then, water was as precious as gold. Suddenly, in a valley so arid that the peasants lived the poorest of lives, this column of water had gushed and thenceforth never failed, not even when the island was scorched brown from end to end . . . Experts now said that much of the island's water originated in the Pyrenees and seeped through deep below the seabed. If true, wasn't that in its own way a miracle?

55

He watched the water swirl down one of the main channels leading from the estanque. Further on, there would be other, smaller stone channels and these in turn would feed temporary earth ones. A web of fertility. To own this land! How tragic that almost certainly Beatriz Ruig had never learned to love it for its miracle and not its money.

He returned to the car and drove on until level with a group of women wearing wide-brimmed straw hats, scarves about their necks, and shapeless frocks with long sleeves, to protect them from the sun. 'D'you know where Frederico is?' he shouted through the opened passenger window.

For a while they merely turned their heads and, bent over, stared at him, like animals on all fours. Then one of them straightened up, dropped a handful of French beans into the trug by her side, and pressed her other hand into the small of her back. 'At home,' she shouted back.

There were nine houses, three casetas, and several barns, all set higgledy-piggledy in relation to each other; even from a distance it was obvious that every building was in need of repair. Around them, chickens scratched and chased pigeons, a pack of shenzy dogs lay here and there, panting, ignoring the Muscovy ducks and two lolloping rabbits. As he stepped out of the car, the dogs came to their feet, barking wildly, the rabbits ran, the pigeons took to the air and made for the pigeon house, and ducks and chickens ignored the sudden turmoil. Time slipped by. A townsman would have become convinced that there was no one in any of the houses and left. He was a countryman and continued to wait.

An old man, face lined and leathered, chin grey with stubble, thickset body slightly bowed from a lifetime of hard labour, appeared in the doorway of what was, fractionally, the largest house.

'I'm looking for Frederico Ferrer,' Alvarez called out.

There was no response.

'Are you Frederico?'

'And if I am?' he finally answered in a deep, heavily accented voice.

'Then I'd be grateful if you've time for a word.'

Ferrer was plainly surprised by Alvarez's friendly manner. 'What about?'

'The señorita.'

'You're the other detective?'

'That's right.'

'From the Peninsula?'

'Do I sound like I am?'

Ferrer brought a pipe from his pocket and put it in his mouth, but did not light it. It was many, many years since Alvarez had seen such a pipe. It was home-made and extraordinarily clumsy, yet it was its clumsiness which attracted him because it lifted him back in time to his childhood when his father had smoked such a pipe, being unable to afford to buy even the cheapest manufactured one.

There was a sound to his left and he half turned, saw between two of the houses a man in his middle twenties, unusually tall for a Mallorquin, with a thin, awkward body and a long, slack face possessing a total quality, rather than a particular one, which marked him as of weak intellect. The moment he saw Alvarez's regarding of him, he ducked back out of sight.

Ferrer said, the pipe still in his mouth so that his words were distorted: 'That's Alberto. His mother was from outside.' He took the pipe from his mouth. 'When he was born, I said, whatever you do, don't let him see the fountain before he's a year old. Instead of just listening, she wanted to know why, so I told her, that's the way it is and the way it's always been. She laughed. That afternoon, she took him to the fountain and even let the water touch him. He's been seeing flying cows ever since.'

Alvarez knew that to show the slightest hint of twentieth-century contempt for the belief that a baby's mental state could be altered by the sight of a fountain

57

would be enough to make certain that Ferrer would never tell him anything. He said: 'There's some you can tell and some you can't; and if you can't, you're wasting your breath to tell 'em they're about to fall down a well.'

Ferrer hawked and spat. 'Are you thirsty?'

'As a mountain ewe.'

He said nothing more, but turned and walked round the corner of the house with the slow, methodical gait of someone who had learned long ago to pace himself for a full day's labour. Alvarez followed him. At the back of the house, under the shade of an overhead vine from which hung dozens of bunches of grapes still small and hard, were a table, fashioned from stone, and three chairs. Ferrer went into the house, to return with a crudely made earthenware jug and two mugs.

The wine was as rough as a cow's tongue and tasted of dry, dusty earth. A connoisseur would have spat it out, Alvarez drank it with a pleasure that came from yet again having memories stirred; the wine his father had made had been one of the very few pleasures of life.

Ferrer refilled Alvarez's glass. 'What are you after knowing?'

'Lucía said the señorita has a cousin. I suppose he'll inherit the valley?'

'Like as not.'

'What's his history?'

Ferrer packed the pipe with tobacco from a rabbitskin pouch. He lit it, puffed out acrid smoke. 'Don Gaspar's wife, Doña Teresa, wasn't no breeder. There was Doña Beatriz, then fifteen years before Doña Cristina and that killed her. It was after she died that Don Gaspar as good as left the valley. Before, everything was kept in order; after, he didn't care and spent his time outside . . .

'Doña Beatriz had to look after Doña Cristina and that caused trouble on account of Doña Cristina having a mind of her own. When she was old enough, she left. Married an Englishman and lived in England until she and him were killed in some kind of an accident.'

'She didn't have much of a life, then?'

'When she was living here, she'd laugh at the fountain.'

One day, Alvarez thought, electricity would invade the valley and following it would come television. Then how short a time would it be before their primitive veneration for the fountain turned into contempt for that veneration? And yet was their belief really any more absurd than veneration for the modern icons – money, cars, absurd soap operas . . . ? 'I gather Doña Cristina's son now lives on the island. Did he visit Doña Beatriz very often?'

'Not to begin with. Amelia said as how they was arguing soon after he arrived the first time. Couldn't expect 'em to get on together, could you?'

'Would you know where he's living?'

'Works in a garage in Playa del Covetas, so I've heard.'

'When was he last here?'

Ferrer puffed at his pipe, found it had gone out, put it down on the table. He went to refill his mug, but the jug was empty. He stood, picked up the jug, went inside.

The heat and the wine pressed down on Alvarez's eyelids and closed them. His mind slipped away . . .

'Do your work sleeping, do you?' asked Ferrer.

He jerked himself awake and watched the other sit. 'That's how I do all my best work . . . Did Doña Beatriz have many other visitors?'

'One or two.'

'Would you call her difficult to get on with?'

There was no answer and he realized he'd made a mistake by asking Ferrer directly to criticize Beatriz Ruig. He was not surprised when this question went unanswered. 'I'd best be moving. I've a Madrileño boss who reckons a man should spend his life rushing.'

'Madrileños are fools.' Ferrer suddenly raised his voice. 'Come on, then. He's a friend.' In a low voice, he muttered: 'It's Alberto; Alberto Pujol.'

Alvarez did not turn. He heard the uneven sounds of

someone slowly approaching, then the ungainly Pujol came within his line of vision. He smiled. After a while, Pujol nervously smiled back.

'You want a drink?' Ferrer asked.

Pujol shook his head.

Ferrer, ignoring Alvarez's earlier statement that he was about to leave, refilled the two mugs.

Pujol advanced another hesitant step which brought him fairly close to the table. 'I've seen a black vulture.' His words were initially difficult to understand because he suffered from a speech defect.

'You're lucky,' Alvarez said. 'I've not seen one this year.'

'Who are you?'

'Enrique.'

'Where are you from?'

'Llueso.'

'I can climb better'n anyone.'

'I can't climb at all because heights make me feel sick.'

Perplexed, Pujol stared at him for a while. 'Where's Llueso?' he finally asked.

'In the north.'

'Is it nice?'

'Very beautiful.'

'More than here.'

'It's different. Here is something very special.'

'I saw the three-colour goat today. Are there goats in Llueso?'

'A lot of farm ones, yes. And some wild ones in the mountains.'

'Show me.'

'One day I'll take you to see them.'

Pujol grinned with delight, clapped his hands, wandered off, head nodding. A small white dog, with a curly tail, suddenly appeared to trot by his side.

Alvarez left a few minutes later and was halfway to his car when Pujol appeared and came skipping up to him, the dog yapping at his side.

'Where?'

'Where what, Alberto?'

'Where d'you live, of course?' Pujol's voice was filled with scorn.

'Llueso.'

'Where's that?'

Alvarez pointed.

'Is it nice?'

Alvarez was saved from having to continue to repeat their previous conversation by the approach of a car. A battered green Renault 5 passed them and, trailing a cloud of dust, headed towards Son Abrut. Alvarez squinted slightly as he struggled to read the number before it had gone too far.

'It was here then,' Pujol said.

Satisfied he had correctly read the number, Alvarez asked: 'When, exactly?'

Pujol giggled.

It seemed that something about the car had previously caught, and in part held, the attention of Pujol's scrambled mind; to have done that, there must surely have been unusual attendant circumstances? 'Was it the night Señorita Beatriz died?'

'I saw lots of goats in the mountains.'

'That should bring you luck.'

'Why?'

'You don't know the saying, "A crow for evil, a snake for trouble, a goat for luck"?'

'One of them has three colours.'

'Three times lucky . . . Was that car here the night the señorita died?'

After a while, Pujol nodded as his eyes filled with tears.

'Was it dark?'

'Nearly.'

'Are you certain it was the same car?'

Pujol left in a series of skips and the dog ran by his side, its tail waving excitedly.

Alvarez climbed into his car and drove off. As he passed

through the narrow, steep mouth of the valley and the land beyond opened up, he felt as if he were leaving one world and entering another – but he couldn't be certain which was the real one, which the false.

CHAPTER 11

When a man was forced to eat away from home and in a gastronomically uncharted territory, it was difficult for him to gauge the quality of a restaurant before eating there unless the number of cars parked outside showed it to be very popular. Popularity suggested tourists, tourists meant poor food and ridiculously overpriced wine.

Alvarez left his car and crossed the narrow pavement to read the faded menu in the glass-fronted case. It was written only in Mallorquin and several of the words were misspelt. He peered through one of the panes in the half-glazed door and saw that huge wine barrels lined both long walls, there were no linen tablecloths, and most of the diners had jugs of wine rather than bottles. An excellent omen. He went in. The warm, rich smell of cooking suggested his choice was a valid one. The vino corriente – costing only three hundred pesetas – the sopes Mallorquines, the lomo con col, the baked almonds and banana, and the bill, confirmed it was an excellent one. Filled with warm, self-congratulatory satisfaction, he ordered a Soberano. The owner brought him a glass and poured out a measure that not even he could complain about.

He lit a cigarette, sipped the brandy, and considered the world. How long would it take Traffic to trace the name and address of the owner of the car whose registration number he had given to them before eating? He had used Superior Chief Salas's name in order to claim priority, but the men in Traffic were a slack bunch who thought nothing of taking a couple of hours for lunch. It might easily be late afternoon before they had an answer. In which case, it was only sensible to return home. Perhaps for a brief siesta?

He yawned, reached across the desk for the receiver, dialled Traffic. To his mild surprise, they had the information. Bernard Tait, 3a, Los Periquitos, Port Beca.

Bernard Tait had the ring of an English/American name. Why should such a man be visiting Beatriz Ruig, who had virtually been a recluse and whom it seemed reasonable to suppose disliked foreigners? Because there was a connection between Tait and the newspaper cutting in the strong-box?

Port Beca (the name had only recently been Mallorquinized) was on the north-east coast and, thanks to a new road which ran part of the way, only half an hour away. Much of the drive was through flat or gently rolling land of such poor quality that little of it was cultivated, with the result that there were few houses and it possessed a sense of seldom experienced distance. Two kilometres from the coast, however, there was a range of hills which swept down almost to the shoreline.

Twenty years before, Beca had been the name given to the whole of the narrow area of scrubland between the hills and the coast; now it was the seaside resort that boasted a jumble of houses, bungalows, apartment blocks, cafés, bars, restaurants, shops which sold leather goods, cheap jewellery, tatty mementoes, food, and an infinite variety of alcohol, and that crowning glory of civilization, a discotheque.

Los Periquitos, on the outskirts, was one of six similar blocks and even the well-tended line of palms and flowerbeds could not dilute the suggestion of barracks. Alvarez parked and walked up a gravel path to the main entrance, which lay between a small food and drink shop that cheerfully overcharged holiday makers and a letting agency which sullenly underpaid owners.

There was no lift and he was forced to climb a seemingly endless succession of stairs. He arrived at the third floor breathless and sweating and it took him time to recover. He rang the bell of 3a. The door was opened by a man dressed in short-sleeve shirt, cotton trousers, and sandals. 'Señor Tait?' he asked in English.

'Yes?'

'My name is Inspector Alvarez of the Cuerpo General de Policia.'

'Then this is what is known as an unexpected pleasure!'

Alvarez decided he had already learned one thing – Tait hid behind a smile. 'I should like to ask you some questions, señor, if that will not disturb you?'

'Ask as many as you like. All I can't guarantee is to be able to answer 'em. Anyway, come on in and we'll find out.'

A tiny hall gave access to the sitting/dining-room which had French windows and a narrow balcony beyond. The furniture and furnishing were of poor quality and impersonal taste, suggesting that the flat was rented.

'Grab a seat. And what'll you drink? Gin, whisky, brandy, vodka, or a San Miguel if you're feeling really thirsty?'

'May I have a coñac, please. No soda, just ice.'

'One brandy straight for you, one G and T for me. Shan't be a moment.'

Tait left the room, to return with two glasses, one of which he handed over. He sat, raised his glass. 'Here's to the first; may the first not be the last and the last not be the first.' He drank. 'Now, satisfy my curiosity. Have I been caught parking where I shouldn't?'

'I believe you knew Señorita Ruig?'

'I don't think so. I'm too old to know any señoritas. Or should I say, too old for them to know me?'

The smile had become broader, but the expression in the eyes had sharpened.

'Señorita Ruig died last Thursday night.'

'Very sad.'

'You did not know she was dead?'

'Since I'm very far from convinced I ever knew her

when she was alive, I can be positive I didn't know she was dead.'

'She lived in Canegot Valley.'

'That name rings a bell, but not very loudly.'

'There is a fountain in the valley.'

'Ah, yes, of course! When friends told me about it, I thought they were pulling my leg . . . If you know what I mean by that?'

'Yes.'

'You speak English very well.'

'Thank you. Have you ever visited Canegot Valley?'

'The friends I've just mentioned took me there to prove the fountain really existed. I must say, I found it an extra-ordinary sight.'

'Have you returned there recently?'

'What exactly is the point of asking these questions?'

'I should like to know the answers.'

'Of course. What I'm really saying is, why do you want to know the answers?'

'Your car was seen in the valley yesterday morning.'

'By whom?'

'By me.'

Tait drank. By some subtle realignment of the lines in his face and the set of his mouth, his expression had become one of cunning watchfulness rather than bonhomie.

'I'm interested in knowing why you went to see the señorita?'

'I haven't said I was driving the car.'

'I can testify that you were.'

'Very well. I was.'

'You did not know she was dead?'

'Would I have driven there if I had?'

'You might have wished to convey the impression that you believed her still to be alive.'

'What's that supposed to mean?'

'Why did you wish to speak to her?'

'That's my affair.'

'It has become mine as well.'

'Why?'

'Because I am investigating her death.'

'The maid said she died accidentally. Are you now saying she might have been murdered?'

'At this point I am not trying to say anything definite, I am merely examining all possibilities. So I will ask you again, why did you wish to speak to the señorita?'

'I had something to discuss with her.'

'What?'

'The matter is confidential.'

'Now that she is dead . . .'

'It will remain confidential.'

Alvarez stared through the French windows at the next block of apartments. After a moment, he said: 'When was the last time you saw the señorita?'

'I don't remember.'

'Perhaps the evening of last Thursday, the day she died?'

Tait said forcefully: 'Are you suggesting I know something about her death?'

'I have already explained why I need to ask these questions.'

'I did not go to her place that evening.'

'I believe that that is not true.'

'Believe what you like.'

'Your car was seen driving up to the house.'

'By whom?'

'By one of the men who lives in the valley. It was round about dusk.' Since he'd enlarged Pujol's muddled evidence that far, Alvarez decided he might as well embellish it further. 'He is an observant and intelligent man; his evidence is incontrovertible.'

'He can be a second George Washington, but I wasn't anywhere near Son Abrut last Thursday.'

'Then will you tell me where you were?'

'With my fiancée, for the whole evening. If you don't believe me, ask her.'

'With your permission, I will do so.'

'And without it?'

'May I have her name and address?'

'Mrs Mabel Owen, Casa Moreno.'

'Whereabouts is that?'

'In the urbanizacíon at the back of this place.'

'Thank you, señor.' Alvarez drained his glass, stood. He was about to move towards the door when he checked himself. 'I have just remembered that I have one more question.'

'If it's on a par with all the others, it won't be worth the effort,' said Tait, as jovially as he could.

'Do you work for Señor Sale?'

'I'm retired and thankful that I am. And further to that, I've never met anyone by that name.'

Alvarez left, disappointed that Tait's final denial had been so confidently emphatic that it might well be true, thus making nonsense of the possibility he had constructed from Pujol's muddled memories.

CHAPTER 12

The urbanizacíon stretched a third of the way up the hill and Casa Moreno stood at the end of the highest road. Alvarez climbed out of his car and stared past the house at the sea, as rich a blue as any travel poster dared portray. Time and time again, on the island one suddenly met beauty so intense that it seemed as if one had been permitted to see one corner of heaven ... Hopefully, heavenly architects were far more gifted than their counterparts on earth who designed such mishmashes of inharmonious shapes and different roof levels.

He descended the four steps to the levelled terrace on which the house stood, crossed to the front door and rang the bell. Jacobo, dressed in white jacket, black tie, and dark trousers, opened the door. Alvarez asked if the señora was in.

'What do you want?'

'A word with her. Cuerpo General.'

'Will you come in, señor.' Jacobo's manner had undergone a very rapid change.

The hall, Alvarez judged, was the size of the dining-room at home; the sitting-room almost as large as the whole ground floor. How rich did one have to be to waste money on so grand a scale? As he waited, he studied the paintings, the beautiful antique furniture, the silver, the carpets, and the figurines; came to the conclusion that one had to be so rich that it was wealth beyond the ordinary person's comprehension.

Mabel entered, carrying Bobby who had a pink ribbon tied around his neck. She nodded curtly, sat. The most expensive cosmetic surgery and the most expensive nostrums failed to conceal her advancing years and there was as much pathetic about her as ridiculous.

The Peke yapped. 'Be quiet, Bobby, he's not going to eat you.'

Only the English, Alvarez was certain, could even consider so disgusting a possibility. 'Señora, I have . . .'

The Peke continued yapping. 'Quiet, Bobby! Shush, darling.'

The Peke finally settled on her lap.

'Señora, I am here . . .'

'There's a good Bobby! Mummy's so pleased, you shall have a choc-choc.' Then she said, without bothering to look up: 'The chocolates are on the mantelpiece in the gold box.'

It took Alvarez a few seconds to realize that he had been addressed. He went over to the marble mantelpiece where a large box of chocolates lay between two ivory tusks, carved with exquisite skill to depict, as he realized after a couple of seconds, scenes that might well have come from the Kamasutra. So shocked was he that for one wild moment he wondered if she really understood what they depicted . . . He carried the box across to her.

' She did not bother to thank him. 'Which choc-choc does Bobby want?' The dog waited until she'd lifted the lid, then snuffled his nose across the line of chocolates, eventually licking one. 'That's always your favourite!' She lifted out the chocolate and the dog grabbed and ate it with loud appreciation. She helped herself to another and her pleasure was only slightly less audible.

'Señora, I need to ask you some questions.'

She swallowed. 'Does Bobby want another?' The dog licked a chocolate. 'You can't have that one, it's a chocolate cream and I always have them. Bobby will have this one.' She fed him, then herself.

'Señora, do you know Señor Tait?'

'Bobby, the gentleman wants to know if I know Bernard. Isn't he a funny gentleman.'

'Can you remember if you saw him last Thursday?'

'Bobby, did I see Nunky Bernard last Thursday?' As the dog gazed up at her with bulging eyes filled with expectant greed, she chose another chocolate and popped it into her mouth.

'Please, señora . . .'

Her jaws moved rhythmically. 'Do you know Kiri?'

'Kiri, señora?'

'People say our voices are almost indistinguishable.'

'Indeed. Would you . . . ?'

'My dear departed father asked me never to sing for money, which is why I have not appeared on the concert platform.'

'Señora, did you see Señor Tait last Thursday evening?'

'Darling Bobby, Nunky Bernard comes and sees us every day, doesn't he? He's so very fond of you.'

'Then he was here last Thursday?'

'That was when Ana said she had to go into Palma to be with her mother who'd been rushed into hospital. Servants really are inconsiderate. Nunky and I had to have cold meat. Mummy doesn't like cold meat, does she, Bobby?' She picked out a chocolate and offered it to the dog, who bit off half. She popped the other half into her mouth.

'Was Señor Tait here all that evening?'

'You're not suggesting . . . You can't believe that . . . What would the servants think?'

That it really could be an overrated pastime? 'Can you remember when he left?'

'We listened to lots of records and then I sang a little because he begged me to and it's so difficult to refuse him. And he didn't go until he'd persuaded me to give an encore.'

'So when would it have been by then?'

'Do I dare tell him, Bobby? Will he think me very naughty for staying up so late? . . . Bobby says it was almost one o'clock in the morning.'

'Thank you, señora.' He stood.

'Say goodbye to Bobby.'
He left.

After climbing over the hills, the road straightened and levelled. No longer having to concentrate totally on his driving, Alvarez considered what he'd just learned. Pujol's evidence had been totally muddled and it could not have been Tait's car which had driven up to Son Abrut on Thursday night. So although Tait had known Beatriz Ruig, there was no reason to believe that he had had anything to do with her death. Indeed, there was now reason for believing that he was correct when he claimed that his driving to Son Abrut the previous day proved he'd no idea she was dead ... But if totally innocent, why had he refused to explain what he'd wished to discuss with her since this inevitably raised the inference that the subject was, at the very least, questionable? Did he know something about Leslie Sale? Was he, in truth, Leslie Sale?

Would any man pursue Mabel Owen (not forgetting Bobby) unless he had an ulterior motive? There was no difficulty in judging what Tait's might be – he lived in a downmarket flat, she in a very luxurious house. If he were – or had been, working for Leslie Sale – swindling his victims, uncovered by Beatriz Ruig, exposure by her might ensure that Mabel Owen cast him aside. Murder would be the answer to such a future. A murder carefully planned and carried out, with all eventualities foreseen. In the time it had taken to drive from the flat to the house, Tait could easily have telephoned her and asked her to provide his alibi, adding a plausible reason for his request. She would be eager to help him because he flattered her and flattery was as desirable as, possibly even more than, chocolates; praise for her beauty, her charm, her singing, and often subtly administered through exaggerated affection for the dog ... To be that murderously and falsely clever usually needed experience, so it was possible he had a record. If the personal details on his application for his residencia were sent back to Britain, the police there could determine whether this possibility was, in truth, fact . . .

He had to remember something before his imagination suggested too much. Because a man's mind was disturbed did not mean that everything he said had to be nonsense. Pujol might not have seen any car on Thursday night; he might have seen Tait's Renault 5; he might have seen a car, whether or not a Renault 5, belonging to someone else. Alternatives which brought to mind the fact that the dead woman had a nephew who worked in a garage. Canegot Valley would be a nice inheritance for a garage mechanic.

Playa del Covetas, on the south coast, was a concrete jungle yet not quite so dense as those which encircled Palma; the provincial government's declared aim to raise the island's image by eliminating the worse excesses of development might just be attainable here.

The sixth garage that Alvarez visited, one road back from the front, was typical of how all garages had looked twenty-five years before – a jumble of cars, drums, treadless tyres, rags, oil, tools, and a compressor which worked only intermittently. Prideful owners of new cars went elsewhere; those who preferred skilled attention and the occasional improvisation sought Garaje Vich.

'Cuerpo General,' Alvarez said.

Vich might not have heard. He leaned over the wing of the Fiesta and began to undo nuts.

'I'm looking for a man who works in one of the garages here.'

'What's his name?'

'I don't know.'

Vich straightened up, an oily spanner in one hand. 'From the sound of you, you're from Llueso way?'

'That's right.'

'I've always heard say it's a daft bunch of buggers living up there.'

73

'That's why I feel at home in this place . . . He's half English.'

'Which half?'

'The half that matters.'

'Then he ain't the one that works here because he's chasing the girls, not the boys.'

'You've a mechanic who's half English?'

'So he says.'

'What's his name?'

'Nigel Mason,' he answered, finding difficulty in the pronunciation.

'Does he own a car?'

'And if he does?'

'I'm interested in knowing its make and colour.'

'Has he had an accident?'

'Not as far as I know.'

Vich tapped the spanner on the filthy palm of his left hand. 'It's a Renault 5,' he finally said. He studied Alvarez, his dark brown eyes keen. 'That means something to you?'

'Maybe. Maybe not. What colour?'

'Blue.'

'Where is he right now?'

'Being part English, he's a lazy sod and wants time off every week. Like as not, he's on the beach with his women.'

'Any idea whereabouts on the beach?'

'Maybe at the far end, by the light. There ain't many tourists get there, seeing it's a way off, and he won't be wanting onlookers.'

The shoreline curved to a very long radius and ended in a spit of land on which stood a navigation light set on a tripod. A couple of hundred metres short of the light, Alvarez saw a parked blue Renault 5. He braked to a stop. In the twilight, it would not be difficult to confuse blue with green.

He crossed the rough grass, the small sand dunes, and the scattered seaweed and came to a couple who lay, face down, on towels. As he approached, the man turned his head to look up. 'Señor Mason?'

Mason replied in fluent Spanish, his accent only occasionally betraying a foreign influence. 'If your car's blown a gasket, swallowed a piston, or shed the transmission, tell Vich.'

The challenging greeting suited the chunky, rugged features and notably square chin. 'Happily, señor, my car has not blown, swallowed, or shed anything.'

'Then what d'you want?'

'I am Inspector Alvarez, of the Cuerpo General de Policia.'

Mason swivelled round to a sitting position, stood. Diana turned over and, shielding her eyes, said in English: 'Is something the matter?'

'I don't know yet.'

No woman as attractive as she should appear topless, Alvarez thought with an emotion that was filled with regret, yet related to anger. It was not fair to make a man remember his youth with such futile longing. He looked away from her and at Mason. 'You are the nephew of Señorita Ruig who lives at Son Abrut?'

'Yes.'

'You have heard the sad news that she died last Thursday?'

'Good God!'

Diana, unable to follow what had been said, but able to judge from Mason's tone that something unusual had happened, spoke quickly. 'What is it?'

'He says Aunt B. has died.'

'The poor old girl!' She came to her feet. 'Still, she was a fair age.'

'She looked as old as the hills, but what she really was I suppose only she knew. So there goes my last near relative.'

'Has he come to tell you when the funeral will be?'

'No date can yet be fixed for the funeral,' Alvarez said in English.

Mason swung round. 'Why didn't you say you spoke English?'

'Why should he when you can understand Spanish perfectly?' Diana said, worried that he had sounded so belligerent. She spoke to Alvarez. 'I thought that because of the heat, funerals had to take place as soon as possible?'

'Normally that is so, señorita.'

'Then why isn't Aunt B.'s?' demanded Mason roughly. 'And come to that, since when have detectives started announcing deaths?'

'A detective?' Diana's voice was sharp.

He didn't answer her.

'It sometimes becomes our duty because we need to ask certain questions,' Alvarez said quietly.

'What questions?' snapped Mason.

'I think this is perhaps not the best place to explain. I suggest we find somewhere else to talk.'

'I'm not moving until I know what the hell this is all about.'

'Why don't we go to Café Toni?' suggested Diana.

76

'Why the devil should we?'

Mason's temper obviously had a short fuse. As a matador would describe it, Alvarez thought, a bull's best friend.

She asked: 'Is your car near here?'

'It is parked next to the señor's.'

Mason said tightly: 'How d'you know which is my car?'

'It's probably the only one nearby,' she said. 'I'll put some clothes on and then we'll go.'

Alvarez studied the horizon and tried to think elevating thoughts, but the sound of material sliding over smooth skin kept them distinctly earthbound. Did a man have to die, he asked himself angrily, before the torment ceased?

'I'm ready,' she said.

For the first time he was able to look at her without a sense of guilt. She was the most attractive of women, perhaps because instead of flawless perfection, there was the flawed joy of golden-red hair in disarray, eyes of a vivid blue that matched the sea a shade too far apart, freckles, a retroussé nose, lips a shade too generous that smiled so quickly and easily . . .

The Renault led the way inland and, as often happened on an island of contrasts, they were hardly out of sight of the sea before they were in the world of winding lanes, small fields, dry-stone walls, and unreformed buildings.

They parked in a village of narrow, winding streets which largely lacked pavements; where the ground floors of many of the houses were shops or workshops; the square was the main meeting place for old as well as young; there was still a public fountain and a public washplace for clothes; and the church bells tolled each death.

Tables were set outside the bar of Café Toni and at one sat four old men, playing dominoes. All four showed their disapproval when Diana in her shorts followed the other two inside. The interior was as dated as the attitude of those outside. On the walls, painted a dreary brown at some time well in the past, hung yellowing prints of bullfighters, there was a sprinkling of wood shavings on the floor, the row of bottles offered only a limited choice, and the owner, chin heavily stubbled, might have grown up leaning on the bar. Only the chrome coffee machine spoke of modern times.

She said uncertainly: 'I do hope you don't mind coming here. I know it looks a bit, well . . .'

Mason roughly interrupted. 'I don't suppose he spends his time at the Ritz.'

Alvarez reassured her. 'Señorita, when I have the choice, I always come to somewhere like here rather than somewhere smart.'

She smiled, a shade nervously. 'I thought you were that kind of a person or I wouldn't have suggested it.'

The compliment gave him an absurd degree of pleasure.

'All right, so how about you saying why we are here?' Mason said.

'First, señor, if you would like to sit, I will get some coffee. And perhaps you would like a coñac as well?'

'Nothing for me.'

'We'd love just two coffees,' she said.

Alvarez crossed to the bar and ordered three coffees and one Soberano. In a tone of satisfaction, the owner said there was only Fundador. He was annoyed when Alvarez was not annoyed. He gained his revenge by not offering a tray and, when one was requested, providing the oldest he could find.

Alvarez carried the tray to the table, handed round the coffees, sat. He drank a little of the brandy, a quarter of the coffee, tipped the remaining brandy into the cup.

'I wish I could draw,' Diana said. 'I'd love to get his character down on paper.' With a nod of the head, she indicated the owner behind the bar.

'You'd have to be Michelangelo to nail all his bloody-mindedness,' muttered Mason.

'That's what's so wonderful about him.'

She understood! Alvarez thought. All the time there were such characters, the island's identity would survive, however many hundreds of thousands of tourists polluted the shoreline.

Mason leaned forward. 'You've got us here. So why? What sort of questions?'

'Questions concerning Señorita Ruig's death.'

'Well?'

'For instance, how exactly did she receive the blow to the back of her neck?'

'Christ! Are you now saying she was murdered?'

'At the moment, the most likely explanation for the bruise is that she fell on to one of the corner posts of her bed.'

'An accident? Why mess up my afternoon for an accident?'

'Nigel!' Diana said worriedly.

'For God's sake! Getting time off from that old bastard back at the garage is worse than drawing teeth. So what happens when I succeed? We're enjoying the beach and then a comedian of a detective has to come along and drag me away because Aunt B. accidentally fell on the corner of her bed.'

'Señor, I did not describe the fall as accidental. That was you.'

'Then you are saying she was murdered?'

'I can only know that when all the questions are answered.'

There was a silence.

'Did your aunt have many visitors?' Alvarez finally asked.

'She was almost a recluse.'

'How long have you lived on the island?'

The change of subject perplexed Mason and it was some time before he said: 'Just over a year.'

'At first, you visited her very seldom.'

'Are you asking or telling?'

'People in the valley say that that is so.'

'Then who am I to deny it? ... I didn't see much of her.'

'For any particular reason?'

'Because from the moment we met, she made me feel as welcome as the tax man.'

'But presumably things have changed recently since you visited her several times?'

Mason finished his coffee, put the cup down. 'More gossip from the fields? . . . She suddenly realized I was her nearest blood relative.'

'Then there's a chance you are her heir?'

'The same chance as my winning El Gordo when I don't buy a ticket.'

'How can you be so certain?' Diana said. 'Don't you remember telling me that in Spain family means everything when it comes to inheriting?'

He spoke harshly. 'Yeah, I remember. It was when I'd had such a skinful I was soft enough to dream there could be a time when your parents stopped looking down their noses long enough to see me. You think Aunt B. would leave anything to the son of a sister who bucked her authority and cleared out to marry a foreigner – a worse family disgrace than marrying a tribe of bastards?'

'People do change,' Alvarez observed. 'After all, although at first she didn't want to see you, she suddenly recognized in an emotional sense that you were her nearest relative.'

'She was getting really old. The really old like to think they'll be remembered by someone for at least a couple of days.'

'What more certain way of achieving that than to name you her heir?'

'If I'm in her will, it'll be as a footnote.'

'You've no idea what the contents of it are?'

'How the hell can I?'

'It will be a valuable inheritance. There's nowhere on the island grows sweeter fruit and vegetables.'

'So what use is that in this day and age?'

'A man can gain tremendous satisfaction from growing fine crops . . . Did she ever discuss money with you?'

'She had a regular moan that she couldn't afford to live.'

'Did she ever mention a Señor Sale?'

'Not to me.'

Alvarez finished his coffee. 'I have just one more question. Will you tell me where you were last Thursday evening.'

'Why?' he demanded angrily.

'Nigel, don't you think . . . ?' Diana began.

He silenced her with an angry wave of the hand. He faced Alvarez, his pugnacious anger very evident. 'Are you saying I killed her?'

'No, I am not.'

'Too bloody twisty to be that direct? If you're not, why so interested in me being her heir? And why bother where I was when she died?'

'In a case such as this, every possibility has to be considered, however unlikely.'

'Then suppose you consider this. I don't give a shit what money she had or who she's left it to. I don't run after people in the hopes of getting something out of them.'

'Then you are to be admired, since that is what appears to keep so many people running . . . Perhaps now you will tell me where you were that evening?'

'It hasn't occurred to you that if I don't know anything about what happened to my aunt, it doesn't matter where I was?'

'For heaven's sake, Nigel, stop being so stubborn!' Diana said. She turned to Alvarez. 'He was with me.'

'Until what time, señorita?'

'I don't know exactly. It was very late because my parents were away for the night and we had the house to ourselves and watched some tapes.'

Watched tapes? When they were on their own? The young of today were so totally spoiled that they didn't have to seize every last chance that was offered them.

*   *   *

81

Dolores began to fidget with her knife, a certain indication that she was annoyed. Isabel, Juan, and Jaime, waited nervously, Alvarez seemed totally unaware of the impending storm as he continued to stare down at his plate which was still half filled.

She said: 'Is it so very tasteless, Enrique?'

He did not respond.

'I said, is it so very tasteless!'

He looked up. 'What's that?'

'Perhaps the pork is tough, the beans are not properly cooked, the chorizo is salty, the ham is tainted?'

He pulled himself together. 'It's a masterpiece of a fabada.'

For once she was not to be sidetracked by extravagant praise. 'Then why are you eating so slowly?'

'It's because I was thinking.'

'About what?'

'The case I'm on.' He drained his glass, refilled it, pushed the bottle across the table. Jaime was about to pick it up when he saw that his wife was watching him.

'This case concerns foreigners, doesn't it?' she demanded.

'That's right. How did you guess?'

'And one of the foreigners is a young woman who flaunts her body?'

He rushed to defend Diana. 'Nothing like that.'

'You think you can persuade me to see rainbows in the dark?'

'She's not that kind of person . . .'

'Fiddlesticks! Have I not had to learn from long, bitter experience that when you stare into nothing with a stupid expression on your face and you do not eat the delicious food I have spent all day preparing, it is because you are dreaming of a woman half your age who covers her face in make-up and her body in nothing?'

'She was wearing a bathing costume and her fiancé was there as well.'

She was not to be denied the last word. 'Since when

82

has another man ever curbed your disgusting lusting?'

He hadn't been thinking of Diana with lust, but sadness
– she was such a poor liar.

CHAPTER 14

Alvarez, slumped in the chair in his office, ignored the ringing telephone. Realizing from the questioning that Mason had become a suspect, frantic to protect him, Diana had rushed to provide him with an alibi. Which suggested he did not have one . . .

The valley was worth many millions, despite the drop in value of agricultural land and the dilapidated state of the buildings. To a garage mechanic, even a few millions was a fortune. The perfect motive for murder. So why, he asked himself, was he hesitating to find out the terms of Beatriz Ruig's will? Self-honest to a fault, he knew the answer. If she had made Mason her heir, he became the prime suspect for her murder. Diana would be shattered. The thought of her frightened despair, of the fact that she might illogically hate him for endangering her fiancé . . . He was overlooking many things, he thought, with a sudden uplift of spirit. First, Diana had obviously responded automatically, without thought, and not because she had the slightest reason to believe Mason guilty. That she had believed he could not on his own prove an alibi, probably did mean that in truth he could not. Secondly, although Mabel Owen had provided a firm alibi for Tait, why should she not be a far more consummate liar than Diana? Thirdly, Tait had been visiting Beatriz Ruig with some frequency; why make a mystery of the reason unless there was need to hide the truth? Fourthly, there was the newspaper cutting and the probability that a considerable sum of money was missing . . .

He studied a map and then the telephone directory,

rang those abogados whose offices lay close to Canegot Valley – not so extensive a task as it might have been since there was none to the north because of the mountains. His sixth call struck gold.

'She was one of our clients; a very occasional one. Which was as well since she never paid her account until absolutely forced to,' said Perello drily.

'Did you draw up her will?'

'I think so, but without checking I can't be certain.'

'Would you look, then; and if you did, give me a résumé of the terms?'

'Her death wasn't accidental?'

'I'm trying to establish what it was.'

'That's interesting!' When he realized he was to be told nothing more, Perello said he'd start checking and ring back when he knew what was what.

'It's a very simple will. Everything goes to her nephew, Nigel Mason, the only son of her sister, Cristina . . . He's come into a considerable property.'

'Better to be born lucky than clever.' Alvarez thanked the other, rang off.

If motive really were the father of crime . . . But all the other possibilities had to be checked out. He searched amongst the muddle on the desk and eventually found the note he had made of the details of Tait's application for residencia, which Palma had provided. He phoned the Cuerpo General in Palma, but side-stepped Salas's office and claimed he was acting on the direct orders of the superior chief when asking for a request to England for any known information concerning Bernard Ian Tait. Finally, he phoned the number which had been on the newspaper cutting from the strong-box. When the connection was made, he asked in English to speak to Señor Sale and mentioned the advertisement in *Ultima Hora*.

'I'm afraid my husband's out at the moment, but I'll get him to ring you back as soon as he returns, which shouldn't be long. If you'll just give me your number?'

85

He stared at the past few days' mail and decided there was small point in becoming involved in any more work, so left it all unopened. He sat back in the chair and closed his eyes, the better to consider the various facts . . .

The telephone awoke him with a start.

'My wife tells me you rang earlier, Mr Alvarez, and wish to discuss financial matters?'

Even over the phone, Sale's voice conjured up warm, friendly earnestness. 'That's right.'

'I'll be glad to have a general chat, but I think I should just mention at this point that my advertisement has generated far greater interest than I expected, with the consequence that I have already been asked to undertake a considerable quantity of work.'

'Perhaps I'd better not bother you, then?'

'Mr Alvarez, you mistake me! All I am saying is this. It has always been my policy – and I pride myself that this is responsible for much of my success – to make certain that before I accept a client there is between us that agreement of intention and sense of trust which is so essential to a good relationship and therefore it is going to be necessary to speak to many parties which will inevitably take time. But just from talking to you now, I feel confident that we shall meet no difficulties and time will not be a cause for delay . . . Tell me, how large an investment do you have in mind?'

'I don't really know at the moment.'

'The careful forethought of the natural investor! As one of the early Rothschilds said, "Search for rocks before diving into the water." I think I will be able to show you that there are no rocks, only deep enough water for any dive. Since the art of good investing is timing, the sooner we meet, the sooner I will be in a position to ensure you a high income and excellent capital appreciation. So when shall it be?'

'How about this afternoon at six?'

'A man after my own heart! Identify an objective, then make for it at maximum speed. Do not be surprised, Mr

86

Alvarez, if this time next year you are a far richer man.'

'But perhaps I ought to wait before ordering a Range Rover?'

Sale laughed heartily.

Alvarez disliked most cities because they denied man an identity; one of hundreds of thousands, he became a mere cypher. But although he would never voluntarily visit Palma, when there he did not feel threatened, nor did he suffer the urge to escape in order to make certain he was still himself. He supposed this was because those who lived in Palma had not totally sold out to Mammon; they still found time from emptying tourists' pockets to enjoy life.

As he turned into Calle Pablo Calvet, another car drew out from the pavement to leave a parking space. His lucky afternoon – perhaps he should buy a ticket from ONCE, the lottery whose proceeds went to the blind and partially sighted? He parked, set the cardboard clock since this was a blue zone, put this on top of the dashboard where even the most officious municipal policeman could not claim it had been hidden, left and walked the two hundred metres to No. 4. A dentist, a doctor, and a company, occupied the first three floors, private individuals the next seven. He pressed the button for Sale and the front door clicked open to let him inside.

Sale had a round, rubbery, smiling face, was slightly overweight, and was smoothly groomed; his manners were jovially confident, his tongue coated in honeyed velvet. There was a prolonged handshake, a brief reference to the unseasonable hot weather and, as they entered the large sitting-room, the offer of a drink. This was brought in by Mrs Sale who was introduced with gallant phrases. Slim, very smartly dressed, her few pieces of jewellery of obvious quality, she was an elegant advertisement for her husband's successes. After handing across the two glasses, she excused herself on the grounds of having to entertain an elderly Englishwoman who was virtually bedridden and almost blind.

'She's very good to the poor old girl,' Sale said in a low tone as she closed the door behind herself. 'Visits her several times a week even though – she'll never admit this, of course – it is a real penance. Old people can be so demanding. But then it's up to those who can to help those who cannot.'

Alvarez admired the way in which the scene was so carefully being set. He drank and transferred his admiration to the quality of the brandy. It wasn't a Carlos I, but it was of that category.

'I suppose we really should talk a little business! So let's discover something. Are you knowledgeable about investing and investments?'

'I know nothing about either.'

'You will probably be surprised if I say that that is an advantage!' He chuckled. 'We have an English poet, Pope, who wrote, "A little learning is a dangerous thing . . ." Before one actively enters the world of financial investments, one must have not a little learning, but a great deal; and one must have one's fingers on the pulses of all the world markets.

'I offer skilled management to all those clients I agree to accept, irrespective of the size of their portfolios. I have never believed that those with considerable investments are entitled to greater consideration than those with lesser ones. The investment strategy for all my clients will be the same although, of course, tactics may slightly differ. An investor with a large portfolio will often be ready to accept greater risk in pursuit of greater profit. But . . . a very great but, this! . . . when I talk about risk, I certainly do not mean risky. For me, risk means a one in ten chance of only slight loss to be balanced against the very much better odds for considerable gain. Last year, I investigated an Anglo-American company called Damon Ushant and came to the conclusion that it had excellent management and a future strategy that held out every chance of success. Although there was a risk that certain contracts might not materialize, in the event, they did. Only a week ago, I sold out one client's holding in that firm at a hundred and ten per cent profit. One cannot complain at that, can one?'

'I doubt I would.'

'So on what terms do we set up your portfolio, Mr Alvarez? Although you mentioned over the phone that you cannot be specific about the capital available, you will have a rough idea of the total and that will enable me to propose a preliminary target. Are we talking about ten million, twenty million, fifty million?'

From the moment he'd read the newspaper cutting, Alvarez had suspected that Sale was a conman; the suspicion had been turned into a certainty by the manner in which Sale's wife had subtly stressed the fact that the family's motto was service and by Sale's smooth, warm, friendly, confidential manner. 'I suppose I could find ten thousand.'

'You obviously keep your money offshore in sterling. Very wise of you! Spain is not a good investment area at the moment; socialism and capital make bad bedfellows. Ten thousand . . . We'll call that two million. Not, of course, as much as I normally . . .'

'Ten thousand pesetas, not pounds.'

Sale's expression sharpened, but he spoke lightly. 'You have an English ironic sense of humour!'

'It's a flattering thought, but unwarranted. Ten thousand pesetas is my entire capital until the next pay packet.'

'Then why the devil have you come here?'

'To ask a few questions.'

'Who are you?'

'Cuerpo General de Policia.'

Sale was shocked. But with the resilience of an old pro, he fought back. 'You've been masquerading as a potential investor when you're really a detective? I thought the secret police had been disbanded.'

'There is nothing very secret about me.'

'Or knowledgeable. Under European Union rules, I am allowed to work here as an investment counsellor.'

'I am not here to dispute your authority to work, but

89

to talk about the investments of one of your clients.'

'Who?'

'Señorita Ruig.'

'Her! It was a bloody thankless day when I agreed to help her! On the phone complaining every time the market goes down even half a point.'

'At least you'll be spared that annoyance in the future, won't you?'

'Why d'you say that?'

'You didn't know she died last Thursday?'

'She died? . . . How could I know?'

'That's what interests me. Perhaps by the sudden cessation of complaints?'

'I merely remarked the silence with gratitude.'

'How much did she give you to invest and when?'

'My clients' affairs are confidential.'

'But yours aren't.'

'Suppose I refuse to say anything?'

'What you say must be your decision. What happens now is mine. I should prefer to be given the information here, in this flat, but if necessary it will be down at the post.'

There was a long silence during which Sale repeatedly looked very briefly at Alvarez, trying to judge how serious was the threat. But Alvarez possessed the peasant's ability of revealing nothing through his expression other than a suggestion of stubborn, uncomprehending vacuity – a suggestion which Sale had sufficient wit to recognize was false. 'She got in touch with me at the beginning of last year and gave me four million to invest,' he said sullenly.

'How much are her shares worth today?'

'I can't answer that without valuing her portfolio.'

'You will have a good idea of the figure since you are, as you have assured me, a skilful, conscientious adviser and investor.'

'Call it three and a half million, depending on the rate of exchange.'

'Most of her shares are in foreign companies?'

'Of course.'

'And despite that, you have lost her half a million pesetas?'

'Only on paper.'

'I doubt she understood the meaning of that. I imagine she became very, very worried; so worried, in fact, that she threatened to report you to the police. And had she done so, resulting in your affairs being closely investigated, you would surely have been exposed as either a swindler or an incompetent adviser. Or, more likely, both.'

'You've no right to insult me.'

'Then the world's stock markets are not standing higher now than they were a year ago, as I read only yesterday?'

'That doesn't mean every single share's gone up.'

'You have managed to buy for the señorita only those shares which have gone down?'

'You're twisting everything. If you knew the first thing about investing . . .'

'Regretfully, since I earn only a village detective's salary, I have little need for such knowledge.'

'Then why make such bloody ridiculous comments?'

'Because I am wondering how, if you are so successful at losing your clients' money, you manage so successfully to guard your own?'

'I . . . Some investments have done better than others.'

'And purely by chance yours are all in that category? Are you sure, señor, that that is the true story? If you were truly concerned about your clients, wouldn't you make certain they shared your successes rather than suffered your failures? It makes me wonder if you are, perhaps, not the rich, successful man you present yourself to be, but rather someone who lives a rich, successful lifestyle because it is financed by money belonging to others.'

Sale, despite the air-conditioning, was beginning to sweat.

'Were that so, of course, the señorita's threat to expose you would have been disastrous.'

'She never threatened me.'

'No? A woman who was a miser, who gloated over every single additional peseta, who believed you would double her fortune only to discover it was becoming less and less . . . Crazed with panicky fear and fury, she will have threatened you. And you, finding yourself on the edge of disaster, must frantically have searched for a way of escape. But there was only one way, wasn't there?'

'What d'you mean?'

'To prevent her exposing you as a conman and a thief, you had to kill her.'

'Christ, you're crazy! I've never killed anyone.'

'Then prove you did not kill the señorita.'

'How can I prove a negative?' Sale shouted wildly.

'By telling me where you were last Thursday night?'

'Here.'

'On your own?'

'Mandy was with me.'

'Will you ask the señora to come in here and verify that fact?'

'She's with the old woman, reading . . .'

'We both know that she is not. That was said to create a good impression.'

Looking slightly sick, Sale stood and hurried out of the room. When he returned, he was accompanied by his wife.

She was no longer assured and even her accent had slipped. 'We were both here,' she said with sharp urgency.

'Is there anyone else who can confirm that you were?'

'Don't you believe me?'

'Señora, I have found it safer to disbelieve everyone until I can believe them.'

CHAPTER 15

The hill was sugar-loaf in form, a kilometre long and almost as wide. It had been virtually valueless because weed grass only grew with difficulty on its rocky, level top and even after the foreigners began to pay ridiculous sums for land, neither of the two families who together owned it had considered it to be worth anything much since it lay eight kilometres inland and everyone knew that the crazy newcomers only wanted to be near the sea.

It was a retired jerry-builder from Bournemouth who had realized the potential of Puig Torre. He had made friends with the two families and found them so accommodatingly naïve that they truly did believe it was man's duty to think of others before himself. Judging the measure of their simple yet deeply held religious beliefs and risking the possibility that, being peasants, beneath their naivety they possessed a hard core of pragmatism, he had concocted a story that was designed to catch and hold their sympathy. He had, he confessed to them, been born of atheistic parents and so as he grew up had discovered his life lacked something, but could not identify that something. Then, only six months before retiring, he'd been on a trip to Damascus (his listeners had drawn in their collective breaths) when suddenly his heart and mind had been opened to the light. He must search for God. And because he had been deaf for so long, he must search alone and in solitude. At the end of the twentieth century, solitude was a rare and precious thing; on this island, where friends insisted on becoming constant companions – no doubt to hide from themselves the barrenness of their lives – it was almost non-existent. Which was why he had so often looked up at Puig Torre and thought with longing that there a man might at last discover what he sought.

The two families had hurried to assure him that he was free to climb the hill whenever he wished and to spend as long on it as he needed. Sorrowfully, he had confessed that, however absurd this might seem, he could never find true solitude on another's property; he had tried, he had failed, again and again. If only the puig was his! He would spend all day on it, searching, listening, learning . . . He was far from a rich man, but would willingly spend every penny he possessed to discover what he sought. A voice within him said that on the puig he would find . . . Was it possible, could it be possible, that they were so filled with the spirit of living brotherhood that they would sell him the puig; that they would help him complete his odyssey and reach Ithaca?

They had hesitated for a long time because, as would any farmer, they were very reluctant to lose even valueless land. But in the end they had agreed to sell to him, the overriding reason for their decision being the knowledge that they would be helping a troubled man to find God.

Over a celebratory lunch, the builder had made his guests laugh immoderately by his descriptions of the stupid peasants who had let a fortune slip through their hands.

He was a clever man and understood that while snobbery was to be publicly deplored, privately it should never be ignored. When selling plots of land on top of the puig, he emphasized the fact that since each cost a minimum of a hundred thousand pounds, and a reasonable house would cost another two hundred thousand, those who chose to live there would not be at risk of suffering as neighbours the little suburban people who were increasingly forming the majority of those who moved to the island to become permanent residents. Such a guarantee was irresistible. Every plot was sold within two years. The builder moved to Guernsey where, to his regretful surprise, he discovered that people of his ilk had been there before him.

For Alvarez, the drive up to the top of Puig Torre was a nightmare. The road zigged and zagged and inevitably he repeatedly found himself on an outside bend with a sheer drop to his side. His altophobia went into hyperactivity and by the time he reached the top, he was sweating almost as heavily as if he had walked.

Ca'n Varney was a vast, ranch-style bungalow in the shape of a U, with a clover-leaf swimming pool enclosed within the wings. Untold lorryloads of prime earth had had to be brought up to make the garden; untold lorryloads of water were needed to maintain it and to keep the pool topped up. The mind was stunned by attempting to work out what it all cost.

Pablo showed him into the sitting-room. As he looked around at the furniture and furnishings, he realized that there truly were people for whom money was no object.

The Grenville-Varneys came through the second doorway and he introduced himself. They replied with the brief, condescending politeness which had he been better acquainted with the finer points of English social manners he would have understood pinpointed the immense gulf between them and him.

Grenville-Varney stood with his back to the fireplace. 'I understand you wish to speak to our daughter?' he said, as his wife sat.

'That is so, señor.'

'Why?'

'I am conducting an investigation and she may be able to help me.'

'Extremely unlikely,' said Lavinia.

'Señora, I can assure you . . .'

'Your assurances are unnecessary.'

England had had an Empire because the English men

had fled the English women. 'Señora, I would not trouble you unless . . .'

'It will save time if you will explain what possible reason you can have for thinking she may in any way be able to assist you.'

'She can confirm that she was in the company of Señor Mason last week.'

'Mason!' Lavinia said.

The Grenville-Varneys looked at each other. Alvarez tried to understand the significance of that look, but could not.

'Why d'you want to know that?' Grenville-Varney asked.

'Because if she can confirm she was with him, I can close one line of investigation.'

'You use the word "confirm". If you understand its true meaning, that suggests you have already spoken to her on the subject. Have you?'

'Yes, señor.'

'Where?'

'I needed to have a word with Señor Mason and the señorita was with him.'

'Is your main concern with Mason rather than our daughter?'

'That indeed is the case.'

'He is in some sort of trouble?'

'I do not know. I am hoping that your daughter will confirm that he is not.'

'What sort of trouble is it this time?' Lavinia demanded.

'Señora, permit me to reply with a question of my own. What trouble has he been in previously?'

'I am hardly likely to know that.'

'From the way you spoke, I thought that perhaps you did . . .'

'You thought incorrectly. What has he been up to?'

'At the moment, I do not know that he is guilty of anything. Indeed, even if your daughter is unable to confirm she was with him, there still will be no certainty.'

'You appear to be singularly uninformed.'

'Señora, in my work it often takes considerable time to become well informed.'

'Then would it not have been more reasonable to have taken that time before coming here and bothering us?'

'Unfortunately, time is always at a premium.'

'So, clearly, is forethought.'

'Señora, if possible I should like to speak with your daughter now.'

They again looked at each other, their expressions once more tantalizingly incomprehensible to Alvarez, then she stood and swept out of the room, trailing an air of exasperation. Grenville-Varney stared into space, making no attempt to conduct a conversation, polite or otherwise.

Diana entered, closely followed by Lavinia. It was very difficult, Alvarez thought, to accept that they were daughter and mother. Was there in this relationship the hint of future imperfection in Diana? It was a tragic possibility.

'Mother says you want to ask me something about Nigel?' Diana said nervously.

'Señorita, I just need you to confirm that you were with Señor Mason last Thursday evening.'

'I told you I was.' She sat.

'Throughout the evening he was with you?'

'Yes.'

'Did you say last Thursday evening,' Lavinia asked sharply.

'That is so, señora.'

'Mason was most certainly not in this house then.'

'Yes, he was,' Diana said hurriedly. 'You were away for the night, staying with Meg and George.'

'We were with them Wednesday night. On Thursday, the Hamptons came to dinner and because they insisted on bringing that daughter of theirs, I asked you to stay at home to try to entertain her.'

'Mother, you must remember, it was Wednesday when the Hamptons were here and Thursday you stayed with Meg.'

She had placed too much emphasis on the word 'must', Alvarez thought sadly.

Lavinia spoke to her husband. 'Which day did the Hamptons come to dinner with that stupid, clumsy daughter?'

'Couldn't say; not very good on dates,' he replied briefly.

'Then if we're to bring an end to this absurd argument, I'll have to get my social diary.' She stood, left. Diana looked as if she was about to follow her, then sank back in the chair, an expression of bitter helplessness on her face.

When Lavinia returned, she carried a large, leather-bound, gold-embossed diary. She sat, opened it, turned a couple of pages. 'Thursday the tenth. Hamptons to dinner. Stephanie's dress sense as lacking in *ton* as ever; Mary bereft of any social graces. Smoked salmon, steak, lemon meringue pie. Salmon Spanish, not Scottish, hardly edible.' She shut the diary.

'Señorita,' said Alvarez sadly, 'were you here at your parents' dinner party on the evening of last Thursday?'

Diana, her face turned away, finally nodded.

'And Señor Mason was not present?'

'They think he eats peas with his knife. He doesn't, he uses his fingers,' she shouted, as she came to her feet. She rushed out of the room, slamming the door behind herself.

'Many a true word is spoken in jest,' said Lavinia.

'Why did you wish to know if our daughter could furnish Mason with an alibi?' Grenville-Varney asked.

'His aunt, Señorita Ruig, died that night.'

'Murdered?'

'That has yet to be established.'

'Hardly surprising, since in this country nothing ever is.' Lavinia said even more pointedly: 'You wouldn't be here, however, asking the questions you have, unless you are reasonably certain she was murdered.'

There could be no denying that.

He stood. 'Thank you for your kindness.' Sadly, he

doubted that they would appreciate the irony of his words.

'I think we handled that rather well,' said Grenville-Varney.

'Even though it took that silly little man an extraordinary time to understand ... So Mason is the complete rotter I have always held he was!' said Lavinia with deep satisfaction.

'I wonder if he did murder his aunt – sounds rather incestuous, doesn't it? Remember, old girl, my saying only a few days ago that a horse with bad breeding will never jump cleanly? ... This calls for a little celebration. I'll fetch that last bottle of Krug.'

Alvarez walked through the press of tourists to Garaje Vich. Mason and Vich were on opposite sides of the opened bonnet of a Citroën GS and the problem they faced appeared to be an intractable one to judge by the inventive swearing.

Vich looked up. 'Well?'

'I've come to have a word with Señor Mason.'

'Señor? He's just my assistant and a bloody useless one at that.'

Having understood the Mallorquin, Mason said in Castilian: 'Pay a peon's wage, you get a peon's work.' He stood upright. 'I said all there is to say yesterday.'

'I think not,' Alvarez replied.

'If you want a chat,' said Vich, 'you can wait until the job's finished.'

'If he's so useless, you'll get on better without him.'

Vich swore with fresh imaginative imagery.

After Mason had changed out of overalls, Alvarez led the way up the road to his parked car. 'We'll drive to somewhere quiet.'

'Drive to John O'Groats and it won't make any difference.'

Alvarez parked by the stretch of beach where he had spoken to Diana and Mason the previous day; memories often had a psychological effect far greater than might be expected.

They sat on one of the sand dunes that was half covered in tussock-grass. Mason was the first to speak. 'Why the hell have we come here?'

'Earlier, I visited Ca'n Varney and spoke to Señor and Señora Grenville-Varney.'

'Why take it out on me?'

'I explained that I wished to speak to the señorita . . .'

'You'd no bloody right to do that.'

'I asked the señorita if she would confirm you had been with her all Thursday evening.'

'Which she did?'

'Indeed.'

'You've dragged me all the way here to tell me she's saying today what she said yesterday?'

'To explain that the señor and señora were present at that time. And the señora read from her diary to prove that you were not with the señorita that evening.'

'Well?' Mason tried, but failed, to sound defiant rather than defensive.

'I need to understand why the señorita lied.'

'Isn't that obvious? Even after twenty-two years, Di didn't believe her mother could be such a bitch.'

'That may very well be true, but it does not answer my question. Why did the señorita think it necessary to try to provide you with an alibi?'

'You made it very obvious you reckoned I might have killed my aunt.'

'And she considered that a possibility?'

'Goddamnit, no! She knew it was impossible. But still instinctively rushed to cover me.'

'Because she is very fond of you?'

'That's our business.'

'Why did you visit Señorita Ruig when you first lived on the island?'

'Because my mother . . . She was always saddened there'd been the complete family breach and had hoped her sister would understand why she'd left home and why she'd married a foreigner . . . Her letters were never answered. Just before she died, she asked me to come here, see my aunt, and explain how much she had longed for a reconciliation.'

'How did your aunt react when you told her that?'

'For all the response she gave, the news of my mother's death and of her wishes were as interesting as last year's weather.'

'You didn't see your aunt again for a long time, did you?'

'Would you have done?'

'Yet recently, you visited her quite frequently.'

'Who says?'

'The villagers.'

'All right, I did start seeing her.'

'Why?'

'She was my aunt.'

'You've just explained why, even though she was, you'd no wish to have anything to do with her. Perhaps the change came when you discovered you were her heir?'

'I told you yesterday, I don't know who the hell's her heir, only that it's a thousand to one I am not.'

'The odds are far too generous. I have spoken to her solicitor and you are named her heir.'

'You . . . you're not pulling my leg?'

'No.'

Mason stared out to sea. 'Good God! Family did mean something to her after all! I'll believe in Santa Claus from now on.'

'You still wish to say you did not know you were her heir?'

'Isn't that obvious?'

'Then why did you suddenly start seeing her if not to ingratiate yourself so that she would not change her will?'

Mason switched to Spanish. 'Maybe you'll understand me now. I did not know I was her heir.'

'The señorita's parents would assuredly look more favourably on a man of property. You had much to gain if you remained your aunt's heir. Equally, much to lose if you did not. Perhaps on your last visit you learned she was about to disinherit you and in desperation you killed her?'

'Christ Almighty! What do I have to do to convince you?'

'Explain why you suddenly started to visit her.'

There was a long silence. Then Mason said, his tone uneasy: 'It's difficult . . .' He became silent.

'However difficult, I assure you that it is very necessary.'

'All right. The garage services the cars of one of the larger hire firms in Playa del Covetas because the man who runs that is a cousin of Vich and doesn't mind what the place looks like so long as the work's OK. A month ago, we had one of their Seat Pandas in to replace the clutch and when we'd finished, I drove it round to them. There wasn't anyone in sight, so I went into the office to let them know and hand over the keys. The owner's son was on the phone and there were three men, one English, two Japanese, having to wait. They'd been talking amongst themselves, but stopped when I went in. Seeing me in overalls and dirty, they obviously took me for a local and unable to understand all that much English and they resumed talking. Something they said caught my attention and so I listened in.'

'What was that something?'

'One of them mentioned Canegot Valley.'

'In what connection?'

'It became obvious the Englishman was trying to sell it to the two Japanese.'

'When it did not belong to him?'

'He reckoned to be able to buy it from Aunt Beatriz.'

'For what possible reason would two Japanese wish to buy the valley?'

'To build a golf course.'

'Impossible!'

'Haven't you ever read how crazy the Japanese are about golf?'

'Perhaps in their own country.'

'You need to have your firm pay or be a millionaire to join a club in Japan. So for the ordinary enthusiast, it's

103

cheaper to fly to another country and play on a course there.'

Sweet Mary, but this had to be the ultimate madness of mobile man! . . . Certain facts began to marshal themselves in his mind. Applications to build several more golf courses on the island had been submitted to the planning authorities. On the grounds that they would provide added tourist attractions, their construction was to be encouraged. But a golf course needed a tremendous amount of irrigation in the summer and already the extraction of water throughout the island was so great that the water-table had dropped to the point where the coastal wells had become saline. The authorities had delivered a delphic verdict. Any or all the courses could be built subject to the one proviso that their maintenance would not call for the extraction of a single litre of water. It was an impossible condition to meet. Impossible, that was, unless there was a valley in which a four-metre-high fountain gushed day and night, even in the burning heat of July and early August . . .

When Alvarez spoke, his words clearly betrayed his peasant background. 'She would never have sold the valley; not when it has been in the family for generations.'

'You really think a woman like her would begin to stack up a bit of land against a couple of million dollars?'

'Two million?'

'That's the money they were talking.'

Over two hundred and fifty million pesetas. A sum so huge it left a man bewildered yet daydreaming madnesses. Would he, he found himself silently asking, sell his birthright for such a fortune? He refused to answer.

'So now do you understand why I started visiting her?'

'If you were eager to inherit a valley worth perhaps thirty million, would you not be very much more eager to inherit one worth two hundred and fifty million?'

'I've told you a bloody dozen times, I didn't know I was her heir.'

'Then what was your motive for visiting her?'

'I . . .' Mason picked up a handful of sand, let it trickle through his fingers.

'Well?'

'I tried to borrow some money from her,' he muttered, anger at having to make the admission almost covering his embarrassment.

His pugnacious words of the previous day – 'I don't run after people in the hopes of getting something out of them' – seemed to hang in the air. There was much truth, Alvarez decided, in the old Mallorquin saying, 'The man who lauds his principles loudly will always sell them swiftly.' 'You thought you were entitled to share in her coming wealth?'

'You don't understand.'

'Then explain.'

Mason picked up more sand, started to let it trickle, suddenly threw it away. He spoke hurriedly. 'School got up my nose because I wasn't interested in what they were trying to teach me. After leaving, I tied in with a gang of drop-outs who made money where it could be made. Then suddenly I knew I wanted to be an engineer. Sounds daft, but that's the way it happened. So I found out how to go about it and discovered I needed to gain the necessary qualifications before I'd be accepted on a degree course. I said to hell with that at my age. That's when my mother – not my father; he'd washed his hands of me – persuaded me to give it a try. It's funny, but no matter what happened, she never lost faith in me . . . And that made me have faith in myself. I buried my nose in books, got the necessary qualifications, started reading for a degree. But then my parents had a car accident and my father died immediately, my mother some time later. By the time she'd died and all the expenses had been met, there wasn't enough left for me to carry on independently and I discovered that the caring government had ceased to care about students, especially those who were ex-drop-outs like me. She'd asked me before she died to give my aunt her last message, so with nothing better to do, I came out, using the few hundred quid she had left me. Aunt Beatriz wasn't interested, but I liked the life and decided to get a job and save until I'd enough to return and finish the degree. I've always had a natural flair for mechanical things and I speak fluent Spanish, so I offered to work for Vich for less than he'd have to pay a Mallorquin. He couldn't resist! Pretty soon, I'd proved myself and so I demanded the right wage. The old bastard found me too good to lose so he had to give it to me. Even with the extra, it was going to take me years to collect enough capital, but I reckoned to do it . . . Then I met Diana. Inside a week . . .

'Her parents took one look at me and decided to break up the friendship. Some of the things they said hurt Diana so much, I shot my mouth off about what I thought of them and that upset her even more and it seemed we'd no future . . . That's when I learned Aunt Beatriz was selling for two million dollars. I'd never tried to borrow before. Always had contempt for anyone who didn't stand on his own two feet. Only . . . only this was different. As soon as I'd a good job, I'd pay her back, with interest. I went and asked her if she'd lend me the money.'

'Did she agree?'

'Not her.'

'But you kept on asking?'

'Pride takes a back seat when you really want something.'

'Now, of course, you no longer will need to ask anyone for a loan.'__

'Which doesn't make me a bloody murderer. I said, I tried to borrow money. If I'd known I was the heir and intended to kill her, I wouldn't have bothered, would I?'

'Perhaps you wisely decided to try the safe option first and only when that failed decided on a far more drastic action. A Renault 5 drove up to Son Abrut on Thursday evening.'

'It wasn't mine.'

'The señorita was so terrified it was yours, she gave you a false alibi.'

'She did that instinctively, without thinking.'

'Because she understood that you had a double motive? With money, you should be able to win her parents' acceptance if not their blessing; you held your aunt responsible for forcing your mother out of Canegot Valley and into a difficult, hard life . . . You knew the habits of your aunt and of those who live in the valley, so could be certain everyone went to bed very early. This meant you could go to her house with little chance of being seen. And, indeed, you would not have been but for someone who does not always act as others do.'

'It wasn't me.'

'Where was your car then?'

'I —' He stopped abruptly.

There were the sounds of far-off laughter, the slapping sail of a sailboard that had come close inshore, the subdued bellow of a distant power boat, the repeated cawing of a seagull, and if one had very sharp hearing, the whisper of the breeze across the sand.

'Where were you last Thursday evening?'

'Nowhere near the valley.'

'That is not an answer.'

'If I tell you, will you swear not to let her know?'

'I will swear to nothing unheard.'

'The thing is, she . . . Well, she wouldn't understand.'

'Neither will I until you explain.'

'Normally I keep as far away from her house as possible because her parents make me feel I'm HIV positive. But her car was being serviced and although they've two, they wouldn't let her borrow one simply because they knew she was meeting me for a couple of hours before she had to return to dinner. So I went to pick her up, but she was still out with her mother. Her father offered me a drink. Being a bloody fool, I thought this meant he was willing to be more friendly. So I seized the opportunity to explain what Diana's been trying to make them understand, that

I was working as a mechanic only to earn enough capital to return to England and resume studying; that I wasn't being big-headed to reckon that when I had my degree, I'd land a good job; that I hoped he agreed that a man shouldn't be judged by his background, but by what he did with life. He looked at me along that Roman nose and said that equality was an American misconception and, like all their others regarding class and breeding, was a recipe for disaster . . . I stormed out before I shoved his superior teeth down the back of his patrician throat.'

'Even though you expected the señorita to return at any moment?'

'If I'd seen her when I was in that mood, we'd have had one hell of a row because I'd have told her exactly what I thought of her parents. She doesn't have red hair for nothing. And although she can see what her parents are like, she always sticks up for them.'

'Where did you go to?'

'To the back street bar I use.'

'You were there for the rest of the evening?'

'No . . . Look, if I swear I never went within thirty kilometres of the valley, will you believe me?'

'I need fact, not belief. Were you with someone who can verify your whereabouts?'

'I . . . I'd been in the bar for an hour or so, drinking damnation to Diana's father, when a couple of women came in, obviously looking for fun.'

'And?' Even in that one word, Alvarez's growing scorn was obvious.

'I'd just been told I was a piece of social shit. How d'you think I felt?'

'My interest is in what happened.'

'We had a few drinks. We went for a drive and stopped further up the coast . . . You know how it goes.'

'No, I do not.'

'I'd drunk enough to make me want to act like the person her parents thought me. Can you understand that?'

'Happily, I am not required to understand your morals. Give me the names of the women and which hotel they're staying at.'

'Sue and Jane.'

'Their surnames?'

'I never heard.'

'You don't even know what their surnames are?'

'God Almighty, in a case like this you don't exchange calling cards!'

'Forgive my ignorance of the finer points of modern etiquette. Which hotel are they staying at?'

'I left them at the front.'

'Are you saying you do not know which hotel?'

'Look, I'd sobered up by then and just wanted to get rid of them because I was feeling . . .'

'Presumably, "guilty" would be an exaggeration. The only thing left to do, then, is for me to see if any of the hotels can identify them from your descriptions. Assuming you took that much interest in what their faces were like?'

'They were returning to the UK early the next morning.'

'Then it is impossible to verify your story.'

'You think I'd make something like that up?'

'I find it impossible to judge. I trust you do not intend to leave the island in the near future?'

'Are you saying I can't?'

'Since you prefer things to be presented in their crudest form, yes, I am.'

CHAPTER 17

In the nineteenth century, Zamora had written: 'There are those in whom good and evil are so entwined that they have two faces.' Mason had found the strength of character to fight his way out of a disastrous lifestyle; yet merely because of injured pride, he had betrayed the woman he loved.

Isabel and Juan were seated in front of the television, Jaime at the table, a glass immediately in front of him and a bottle within reach.

Alvarez opened the sideboard and brought out a glass, sat, poured himself a drink. He spoke to Jaime. 'Tell me something. Could you love a woman, yet one night go to a bar, meet a couple of tarts, have a few drinks and take 'em off for all sorts of fun and games?'

'Only if I was luckier than I usually am.'

Juan swung round. 'Can't you be quiet. We're trying to watch the telly.'

'If your uncle and me want to talk, we will; is that bloody clear?'

Dolores appeared in the doorway of the kitchen. She said, her voice scornful: 'Is it impossible to speak even to your own innocent children without swearing?'

Jaime pointed at Juan. 'Innocent? You call him innocent?'

'If he has lost any of his innocence that is because he has you for a father.'

'That's right, it's my fault! It's always my fault!'

She spoke to Alvarez. 'The phone has rung four times for you and always it's that obnoxious woman.'

110

'The superior chief's secretary?'

'She told me to speak Castilian. The language of this island is Mallorquin! If she lives and works here, she must speak our language, not hers. Tell her that.'

'I will,' he assured her, managing to sound as if he meant it. 'Did she say what she wanted?'

'Each time I said you were not here, she rang off without even the manners to say goodbye.'

'Something very important must have turned up.' He looked at his watch.

'I am about to serve supper.'

'Then there's no point in ringing back tonight.'

She glared at her husband, vanished back into the kitchen.

'She never changes,' Jaime said mournfully.

He'd no idea how fortunate he was that his wife had only one face.

Alvarez drove through the narrow entrance and the valley opened up. He braked to a halt when abreast of the huddle of buildings. As he left the car, a pack of dogs rushed up and encircled him, barking furiously, chickens scattered but only for a few metres, several pigeons took to the air, and a hoopoe passed with undulating flight.

A woman, dressed in a shapeless, faded frock, appeared in the doorway of one of the houses. 'I'm looking for Alberto,' he told her.

'He ain't here.'

'Where will I find him?'

'In the fields, maybe.'

None of them would volunteer information; it had to be carefully prised out. 'Do you know which end of the valley he'll be working in?'

'Can't say.'

He thanked her, returned to the car, drove along the dirt track and then came to a stop by a group of women who were picking strawberries, backsides high in the air, and asked if they knew where Alberto was. One of them shouted at a man who was using two bullocks to plough a square of land and he called across to another who was planting out sweet pepper seedlings. When the last man straightened up, Alvarez recognized Ferrer.

Ferrer, moving with slow, measured steps, came round the edges of three different crops and up to the car.

As custom dictated, Alvarez shook hands and discussed crops before explaining that he wanted a word with Pujol.

Ferrer, the depths of the lines in his face highlighted by the brilliant sunshine where the brim of the battered straw hat did not throw shadow, shrugged his shoulders.

'He's not in the fields?'

'Only works when he wants to. When he don't, he's usually up in the mountains. There ain't no one tries to tell him what to do.'

In the past, mental troubles had usually been seen as a reason for compassion; beyond the valley, modern values had changed that. 'And you're certain he's not in the fields now?'

Ferrer turned slowly, studying each figure. 'He ain't.'

Alvarez knew better than to doubt the judgement, even though some of the men were so distant as to be little more than indistinct shapes; each worked with a rhythm that was identifiable. 'It sounds as if there's no knowing when he gets back from wherever he is?'

'That's right.'

'Maybe he won't be too long. I need a chat with him so I'll wait around for a while.'

'Suit yourself . . . More'n likely you've still got a thirst?'

'Never lose it.'

He shouted at a nearby woman to take over the planting of the seedlings, climbed into the front passenger seat. Alvarez carried on towards the house for a couple of hundred metres to reach a point where there was room to turn, then drove back to the village. Dogs barked, chickens flustered, pigeons flew, and it was even the same woman as before who looked out to see who had arrived.

Ferrer led the way to the patio of his house, brought

112

out a jar of wine, two mugs, and a small earthenware bowl of olives, which he set out on the stone table.

Like the wine, and the pipe not now in evidence, the olives lifted Alvarez back through the years. They were peppery and bitter, an acquired taste that made the perfect accompaniment for the rough, earthy wine. 'They're good. Who cured them?' He flicked two stones over the wall.

'The wife. Won't be doing no more; died early this year.'

He'd mentioned her death without the slightest show of emotion but this did not mean, Alvarez knew, that he escaped grief; he accepted it because he had not been misled by television and the cinema into the fatal error of believing there was always a happy ending. 'Have you children?'

'We wanted 'em; there wasn't none.'

They heard a scuffling noise and both looked round in time to see the small white dog with curly tail turn and scamper back out of sight.

Ferrer called out: 'It's the inspector. You met him the other day. Come and drink.' He said to Alvarez in a low voice: 'Best not to say too soon you want to ask him questions.'

Almost a minute passed before Pujol sidled around the corner of the house, followed by the dog.

'Get a mug for yourself.'

Pujol began to walk past the table, came to a sudden stop. 'You live in Llueso.'

'That's right,' Alvarez answered.

He thought about that for a while. 'You're going to take me to see the goats.'

'One day soon.'

'Not now?'

'I'm afraid not.'

Pujol's face crumpled. He walked into the house with shoulders bowed, yet when he returned, a mug in his right hand, he was walking with shoulders squared and was whistling. He sat and poured himself a mugful of wine. He reached for the olives, put four into his mouth.

'Where have you been walking?' Ferrer asked.

'Puig Xischa,' he answered, before he spat out the stones.

'Did you see the goats?'

'There was the one with a white patch on its right ear. Then there was the one with . . .'

He had seen twenty-one goats and kids and described each one by its distinguishing markings in what was a considerable feat of memory. Then he talked disjointedly about the ice house on top of the puig. 'The roof's fallen in; why don't you mend it?'

'No one don't use it any more so there's no point,' Ferrer said.

'Why don't they?'

'Because it's hard, cold work to climb up there in winter and collect the snow and pack it down with straw. Who's going to do that when now if you want ice, you buy it?'

'I like ice-cream.' He turned to Alvarez. 'I like chocolate ice-cream.'

'Then I'll buy you some.'

He chortled with glee, drank noisily, reached across for more olives.

Alvarez judged it a good time to say: 'Do you remember the last time I was here?'

Pujol stared at him, frowning heavily as he thought.

'You told me something that interested me very much.'

Pujol was surprised and delighted.

'You told me about the car you'd seen which drove up to the señorita's house the night she died.'

Pujol gestured with his hand, knocked over his mug which broke into two pieces. The wine spread across the stone before being sucked in. He came to his feet, his expression one of fright.

'No call for worry,' said Ferrer easily. 'Plenty more mugs where that one came from. And whilst you're getting it, fill up the jug.'

Pujol hesitated, then picked up the jug and went into the house, followed by the dog. Ferrer picked up the two pieces of mug and threw them over the wall. 'He's been

114

breaking things since he was a kid. His dad used to beat him to make him more careful, but as I said, there just ain't no way of making someone like Alberto careful.'

Pujol returned with a mug and the refilled jar. He sat, poured himself wine and drank.

'You were telling me about the car,' Alvarez said.

'What car?'

'The one you saw the night the señorita died. Can you remember what kind it was?'

Pujol shook his head even as he said: 'Like the cousin's; him what's her English cousin.'

'Perhaps it was his?'

'No.'

'How can you be certain?'

He didn't answer.

'Maybe something about it was different?'

'It were brown.'

Previously, he had said it was green. Perhaps next time it would be all the colours of the spectrum. 'You've a wonderful memory.'

Pujol nodded enthusiastically.

Alvarez had hoped to learn much more than he had. Yet as he refilled his mug, helped himself to more olives, and drank, he felt the peace of the valley and knew he was gaining far more than he could have hoped.

CHAPTER 18

Nothing better underlined the difference between time past and time present than the comparison between the valley and the urbanizacíon in which Los Periquitos stood. Alvarez came to a stop on the second landing to recover his breath and as he wiped the sweat from his brow, he wondered how the architect could have been so stupid as not to plan a lift? A question that highlighted the fact that the past was only truly desirable when viewed through the eyes of the present. Perhaps it was as well that one could never live one's nostalgia . . .

He climbed up to the third floor, rang the bell of flat 3a. There was only a short wait before Tait opened the door. 'Well, well! An inspector calls! Still hot on the scent, deerstalker on head, pipe in mouth?'

Alvarez didn't need to understand the references to realize he was being mocked. 'I need to ask you a few questions.'

'You've more questions than Bobby has fleas . . . I gather you saw Mrs Owen to find out if I was telling the truth?'

'To confirm that you were.'

'A man of tact! Come through where there's a fan on so that there's an illusion of coolness. And these days, illusion has become more real than reality, hasn't it?'

They went into the sitting-room. 'Grab a seat and tell me what you'd like to drink?'

'A coñac, please, with just ice.'

'Also a man of custom!'

After pouring out the drinks and handing Alvarez a

116

glass, Tait raised his. 'Here's to crime – the one recession-proof occupation.'

'Señor, do you remember what you told me when I was last here?'

'Not in detail. But I can assure you that it was the truth, the whole truth, and nothing but the truth.'

'You said that you had conducted business with Señorita Ruig.'

The smile remained on Tait's lips, but left his eyes.

'When I asked you what was the nature of that business, you refused to answer.'

'Not from any sense of apprehension, I assure you. But from the old-fashioned belief that a business dealing automatically creates a strict bond of confidentiality.'

'But you would agree that however strict, sometimes such a bond has to be broken?'

'Only when circumstances produce a situation where there is a greater duty to reveal than to conceal.'

'Circumstances do so now.'

'I omitted one very important proviso. It is a subjective decision, not an objective one. I see no reason whatsoever why I should tell you what was the nature of our mutual interest.'

'It is difficult to imagine what business interest you and the señorita, a reclusive miser, could have had in common if not that she had something to sell which you wished to buy. Perhaps the valley?'

'You are a man of considerable imagination!'

'I will give it full rein. The Ruigs held the land for so many generations that built up in almost all of them was the belief that they and the land had in some sense become one and therefore each held it in trust for the next generation. The señorita must have experienced this belief each time she looked out over the valley, blessed by the fountain. So what could have been so strong as to have overcome that?'

'I've no idea.'

117

'She was a miser. Even greater than her prideful belief was her all-consuming love of money.'

'I mean it as a compliment when I say that you are a man of very considerable, romantic imagination.'

'So if she were offered sufficient money, however loath to sell she would have been on one emotional level, she would have agreed.'

'No one would ever offer much for a load of tumble-down buildings and some agricultural land.'

'They would if they wished to build a golf course and so had to have almost limitless water without drawing it from a well; and if they came from Japan they would offer not a trunkful of pesetas, but many trunkfuls.'

'You really think any Japanese would want to build a golf course umpteen thousands of miles from Japan?'

'I would not, no. But I understand that that merely proves how ignorant of the world I am. To play golf in Japan is to show that one is a big man because only the rich can afford to do so. Since many more wish to be seen to be rich than are, special flights are arranged to take them to play in other countries where the cost is so much less. It already happens in England. Why should it not happen here?'

'You almost make it sound plausible!'

'Were you acting on commission?'

'I did say, "almost"!'

'What are the names of the Japanese with whom you were negotiating?'

'I don't think I've ever met a Japanese.'

'Señor, the more you lie, the more I am led to believe you must have a very strong reason for lying ... You were discussing the proposed sale with two Japanese in the offices of a car hire firm.'

Tait drained his glass. 'I must apologize for trying to mislead you, but I do assure you that my only motive was to try to preserve client confidentiality. Yes, I was engaged in selling the valley to the Japanese.'

'What are their names?'

'Mr Ando and Mr Mizutani. But, of course, they're the front men. The money comes from the Urakawa Company and who knows who's behind that?'

'You were selling on commission?'

'That was my first suggestion. She turned the idea down and said all the money had to be paid directly to her. I don't think she was doubting my honesty – at least, I hope she wasn't. It's just that she wanted it all in her hot little hands at the first possible moment . . . I'll be totally frank now. At this stage, it seemed to me that if the money went to her first, then getting blood out of a petrified stone would be a sight easier than prying my share out of her. So I took the only remaining option and offered to buy the land from her so that I could resell it to the Japanese. After very prolonged haggling, that's what she agreed.'

'What was the price?'

'A million dollars.'

'Have you paid her?'

'She haggled so hard that the contract was signed only very shortly before she died.'

'Where were you getting the money from?'

'Mrs Owen is very kindly lending it to me.'

'So how much are you selling the valley to the Japanese for?'

'A small profit. Which, I would add, will be very hard earned. After doing business with Señorita Ruig, a cross-eyed Levanter would be easy meat.'

'Why are you still lying?'

'What the hell sort of a question is that? I'm baring all my most intimate business secrets.'

'You were selling to the Japanese for two million dollars.'

There was a long pause. 'A man's entitled to make a profit.'

'Of a hundred per cent?'

'Is it against the law?'

'You don't think that when dealing with a woman who

has very little knowledge and no experience of the outside world, one owes her a duty to be totally honest?'

'You obviously don't mix with antique dealers.'

'Do you have the contract?'

'My copy, yes.'

'I'd like to see it.'

After a moment, he stood, left the room to return within the minute.

Alvarez read the contract, dated the fourth. He was no lawyer, versed in the art of identifying ambiguity when none was apparent, so to him it seemed a straightforward agreement. The sum of a hundred thousand dollars, US, to be paid on signature and the remaining nine hundred thousand on completion.

'Are you satisfied?' Tait asked.

'I have still one question.'

'Perhaps I should be grateful that you are so parsimonious.'

'Why is this copy of the contract still in your possession and not with an abogado or notario?'

'Do I really have to point out that on this island, time is timeless?'

'Then you wish me to believe you were not in a hurry to complete the deal? . . . Shall I tell you what I think is far more likely?'

'If you insist.'

'I don't think that Señorita Ruig signed this contract on the tenth.'

'Since it's dated the fourth, you probably are correct!'

'You pre-dated it by six days and forged her signature . . . By nature someone who wanted every last peseta, she bargained with a keenness that you have told me surprised you. Then, before signing, she learned you were selling the land for two million dollars. Naturally, she decided to bypass you and sell directly to the Japanese. That forced you to murder her if you were to gain any profit from the deal.'

120

'And how did I manage to do that when I wasn't any-where near her house?'

'On the contrary, you were present. Your car has been positively identified.'

'A miracle. Since it was outside my fiancée's house all that evening.'

'It was not.'

'You're calling her a liar?'

'Only with the deepest regret.' Alvarez stood. 'I'll have the contract back, please.'

'It will be returned after it has been studied in Palma.'

'Studied for what reason?'

'To learn if the señorita's signature was forged.'

Tait's expression, before he managed to control it, was one of consternation.

CHAPTER 19

After reading the report from England, Alvarez felt sufficiently discouraged to lean over and pull open the right-hand bottom drawer of the desk, lift out the bottle of brandy and glass, and pour himself a generous drink. If Tait had been guilty of violence in the past, he could have been considered that much more likely to have murdered Beatriz Ruig because every act of violence encouraged a man to commit a greater one. But according to the English police, he had no criminal record.

Perhaps, he thought, as the brandy soothed his disappointment, he was reacting with illogical uncertainty. After all, Tait might have been violent without this fact ever becoming officially known; his true character might be that while normally his emotions were under control, his tendency towards violence could be triggered by something as sharp as the loss of a million dollars . . .

He reread the report. Bernard Ian Tait. Married seventeen years; lived at the same address throughout the marriage; a life insurance salesman . . . On the face of things, a typical suburbanite. But it paid never to forget the old adage, 'A smiling face conceals a black heart more readily than a frowning one.' Perhaps domestic violence had been responsible for the break-up of the marriage?

He dialled International Inquiries, asked them to give him the telephone number of Señora Tait who lived at 16, Cawdor Road, Southfields. Ten minutes later, they provided it.

As he dialled that number, he decided that, however unwillingly, Salas was going to have to commend his initiative! 'Am I speaking to Señora Tait?' he asked, when the connection was made.

'My name is Mrs Prescot.'

'But your address is sixteen, Cawdor Road?'

'Yes.'

'Then you can tell me where Señora Tait is?'

'Who are you and why do you want to know this?'

The tone of voice caused him to picture a tall, thin, angular Englishwoman, capable of running a church fête, but not of sharing a night of passion. 'My name is Inspector Alvarez, of the Cuerpo General de Policia.'

'You are a policeman?'

'That is so. I am ringing from Mallorca because I wish to speak with Señora Tait and I have been told that she lives at your address.'

'She did, up until a month ago when we bought the house. I suppose the change of ownership hasn't been recorded yet. People are becoming more incompetent every day.'

'Do you know where the señora is living now?'

'To be frank, we did not exchange confidences, so I've no idea.'

'Did she at any time mention some other part of the country?'

'No.'

'You saw nothing in the house when you first visited it which suggested somewhere else?'

There was a pause. 'Now you mention it, I remember that there were a couple of paintings of Norwich, one of the cathedral and one of the castle, which caught my attention because I have an aunt who lives there. She said that she was born there. I'm afraid that's all.'

'Thank you very much, señora.'

He replaced the receiver, settled back in the chair. Perversely, because he had failed to speak to Tait's wife, he was now convinced she could provide information that would unlock this case. How to find out where she now lived? Impossible! She might have moved to anywhere,

123

either within or beyond the British Isles; she might have remarried and now have a different name . . . He poured himself another drink and his thoughts became more optimistic. Not every woman rushed into remarriage; indeed, Dolores claimed that after surviving one marriage, no sane woman would ever contemplate a second. People were drawn back to where they were born, as if an invisible thread joined them – as Massaneto had written, 'A man's journey through life is a return.' So Señora Tait might very well have moved to Norwich and it was certainly worth asking the English police there to check on the grounds that she was known to have done so (any suggestion of doubt might lead them to conduct a less than vigorous search).

He phoned Palma and, once again using the superior chief's authority, requested that a message be sent to the liaison officer in London, asking for information on the whereabouts of Señora Tait.

He drained the glass, looked at his watch and was gratified to discover that it would soon be time to leave for lunch.

He drove into the valley and spoke to a woman by the houses and asked if either Lucía or Amelia was around? A shout, twice repeated, brought Amelia out of one of the smaller houses.

He greeted her with his usual friendliness, spoke about the endless fine weather and the shortage of water outside the valley, then mentioned that he needed to look through the señorita's house again and would she unlock it for him?

'There's no need. It's never locked.'

Another reminder of the past; a reminder that once upon a time – pre-tourist time, that was – one left the key hanging on the outside of the front door to show that one was out.

He drove on to Son Abrut. As Amelia had promised, the front door was unlocked. He went inside, into a gloom

— all the shutters were closed — which smelled of damp, decay, and perhaps death.

In the study, he opened the shutters of both windows. The sunshine streamed in, restoring a little life. He looked around him. Had the señorita's grandfather walked through the door, he'd surely feel as if he'd last been there only the day before. The room spoke of measured, dignified, fruitful lives; of duties recognized and observed; of unchanging values. Qualities that, tragically, she had rejected . . .

He began his search, more hopeful than confident. He was, therefore, gratified to find in one of the small drawers of the desk what was either a draft or a holograph copy of a letter to Señor Sale, explaining that she had four million pesetas she wished to invest and how much she hoped he would help her. The letter was even signed . . . It was not every day that fate dealt a pat hand. In a flush of enthusiasm, he decided that he'd ask Palma to compare the two signatures right away and not wait until Monday to do that.

Professor Fortunata's secretary telephoned on Saturday morning, much to Alvarez's astonishment, since most of those who worked for the government were convinced followers of the English style, elongated weekend. 'I have the professor's report and will be sending it on, but I thought you'd like a résumé of the facts now since it may take a week, or more, for the post to reach you. Apart from the bruise to the back of the neck, the deceased showed no classic traces indicating the cause of death. Since the bruise was relatively minor, the professor is of the opinion that she died from vagal inhibition. Are you conversant with the term?'

'I am afraid not.'

'It is defined as an exaggerated reflex vagal response to trivial pleural stimuli. Perhaps the term "extreme shock" where the test is subjective and not objective most readily describes it in lay terms. There is a case on record where students conducted a mock execution by guillotine, administered the last rites, and then flicked the victim's neck with a towel; he died instantly. Women have died while attempting an abortion the moment the chosen instrument touched their flesh. Many a prostitute has died when her client, in his passion, put his hands on her throat and she believed she was about to be strangled.'

'Does this mean that the señorita was literally frightened to death?'

'In the sense that something happened which shocked her to such an exaggerated extent that she suffered a fatal response, yes, it does.'

He thanked her, rang off. Beatriz Ruig had had reason to believe she was about to be murdered.

He tried to overcome Monday morning blues by day-dreaming. He'd won El Gordo and in his bank were so many pesetas that the purchase of Canegot Valley hardly registered. Another twenty million to reform the manor house, perhaps fifty million to put all the other buildings in good repair, a couple of million to bring in electricity. The main irrigation channels needed to be rebuilt and covered to prevent loss by evaporation. New crops, offering better returns, must be introduced – avocado pears, limes . . .

The telephone brought him back to the office.

'The superior chief wishes to speak to you,' said the secretary in her plummy voice.

He waited.

'What the devil do you mean by using my name without my authority?'

'I'm not quite certain . . .'

'A condition to which you are far from a stranger. Did you, or did you not, quote my authority for the request to the British police for any known details concerning a Señor Tait?'

'As a matter of fact . . .'

'Did you at a later date once again quote my authority

for information regarding the present address of Señora Tait?'

'It is true that I made . . .'

'You admit using my authority falsely?'

'In one sense, perhaps one might claim that. But knowing how busy you are, señor, my one motive was to save you trouble.'

'If you are still seized by that desire, kindly apply for a transfer to the Peninsula.'

'Señor . . .'

'My God! Not only have you taken my name in vain, you have proved yourself ignorant of the rules of procedure by conducting an investigation into a case without any reference to this office.'

'But you know all about it . . .'

'I will thank you not to instruct me in what I do or do not know.'

'But it's you who detailed me to make the investigation.'

'Alvarez, have you gone mad?'

'I don't think so, señor.'

'Then are you drunk?'

'Of course not.'

'I have not – I repeat, not – told you to investigate anyone by the name of Tait.'

'Directly, that is so, señor. But indirectly you have when you ordered me to investigate the murder of Señorita Ruig.'

'The what?' Salas shouted.

'The murder of Señorita Ruig at Son Abrut on the tenth . . .'

'I knew it! I bloody well knew it! I should never have listened to Garicano. I should not have given you the opportunity to indulge yet again in your perverted delight in confusion. Yet even forewarned by countless impossible disasters, could I really be expected to imagine you could confuse a case already solved?'

'Señor, this case is not quite as straightforward as Inspector Garicano thought it.'

'Of course it isn't. Not now. Not after you have been concerned with it.'

'I have just heard from the Institute of Pathology. The señorita died from vagal inhibition which means she suffered a shock severe enough to cause an exaggerated response which resulted in her death. Obviously, she believed she was about to be murdered and this belief killed her before the murderer did.'

'The professor categorically states she feared she was about to be murdered?'

'What else could cause her so severe a shock?'

'It has not occurred to you that when she fell and hit her head, she reacted with typical female hysteria and became convinced the blow would prove fatal?'

'I don't think that that would come within the definition of extreme shock as applied here.'

'You have medical qualifications of which I am unaware?'

'No, señor.'

'Then refrain from medical judgements . . . Answer me one thing, Alvarez. Have you the slightest conception of what is meant by logic?'

'Yes, señor.'

'Then by what tortured feat of the imagination do you conclude the señorita's death was murder when it could not have been anything but accidental?'

'There are one or two facts . . .'

'All the facts were established by Inspector Garicano. But wait! Perhaps you are trying in a somewhat muddled way to claim that you have uncovered evidence which proves him wrong? Let us discover what that evidence could be. The señorita was not, in fact, in her nightdress?'

'Yes, she was.'

'The door of the bedroom was not locked and bolted?'

'Yes, it was.'

'That leaves only one possibility. The shutters were not firmly secured. I wonder how the inspector – a meticulous man – could have made such a mistake? Still, even Homer nodded. If you will just detail exactly what was his mistake?'

'The shutters were firmly secured.'

'They were? Then we undoubtedly have a problem. How do you introduce a man into this locked and bolted bedroom who threatens the señorita to death and then leaves with all locks, bolts, and bars in place? Perhaps he beamed himself out, Johnnie?'

'Scotty.'

'What's that?'

'Nothing, señor. But one has to remember the candle that was in the room.'

'Enlighten me on why one should.'

'It had been snuffed out.'

'And you find that unusual?'

'The candlestick was not within reach of the bed, yet she died in bed. Would she not normally have kept the candle alight until in bed and settled?'

'Perhaps you might at your leisure consider the possibility that after she had changed into her nightdress, she fell and hit the bedpost and that left her so disorientated that she climbed into bed without worrying about the candle.'

'If that's what happened, the candle would have burned down.'

'There are no draughts?'

'The candle was protected by a glass funnel. There is another important fact. The mobile phone was left downstairs.'

'Perhaps because she knew she'd have no need to make calls during the night.'

'But who knows when there is going to be an emergency? And the older one becomes, the nearer that emergency approaches. But more to the point is the fact that she was a miser and so for her the phone would have cost a fortune. In which case, she would have guarded it as carefully as she could and this meant bringing it up to her bedroom.'

'Old people become forgetful.'

'On its own, the significance of this point could perhaps be dismissed, but when it is viewed in conjunction with others . . .'

'Which can be dismissed with equal brevity.'

'Señor, I have identified three men, each of whom has a motive for murdering the señorita.'

'Since it is impossible there was anyone else in her bedroom, it doesn't matter a damn if there were a dozen men who had motives for killing her. You might like to reflect on the fact that were a motive for murder as good as evidence of murder, I should be in danger of arrest . . . Where is your report?'

'But I haven't finished my investigation . . .'

'That is where you are quite wrong. You have concluded it as from this moment and will cease to meddle in the case in any shape or form. Is that clear?'

'Yes, señor.'

'I was referring to the report I ordered you to make after your initial, general search of the house.'

Alvarez was surprised to discover how completely he had forgotten about that.

CHAPTER 20

'Llueso?' said PC Gill, temporarily attached to CID for plain clothes duties. 'I went there on holiday last year.'

'You aren't on holiday now,' said the detective-sergeant, 'so on your way.'

Gill stared through the window at the grey day beyond. 'Didn't see a cloud in the whole fortnight. Just sun, sea, and sand.'

'No sex?'

'Not out of doors . . . A litre of gin cost under a fiver.'

'If you go on much longer, you'll have me in tears. Get moving and find out where Mrs Tait's living.'

'You know, it's a bit of a tall order. I mean, I'll try the estate agents, of course, and the hotels in case she hasn't bought a house yet and is still looking for one, but . . .'

'Do you know the difference between a parrot and a PC? The parrot sometimes stops talking.'

Gill made his way to the courtyard where he discovered that all the CID cars were out. He swore, but with the good nature with which he did most things. A five-minute walk brought him to the first of the city's estate agents. The blonde receptionist made him think, both nostalgically and hopefully, of Mediterranean islands, but she met his interest with cool indifference. After making brief inquiries, she told him that the firm had not had any contact with a client by the name of Mrs Tait. He left and in the course of the next hour and a half received the same answer from another five estate agents. It was going to be one of those days, he thought. He was wrong. The middle-aged receptionist in the seventh agent returned to

131

the desk and said: 'I have spoken to Mr Dyson and he says that contracts for a property have been exchanged with a buyer called Mrs Hannah Tait.'

'Do you know her present address?'

She handed him a sheet of paper on which she had written, in near copperplate, the name and address of a hotel.

'Cheers! I'll return the compliment one day.'

She was slightly upset by the suggestion that she should ever be in the position where a policeman's help might be necessary.

It was more a boarding house than a hotel and although it was not actually seedy, seediness hovered in the background. After a ten-minute wait, during which he read in a woman's magazine an article on dream men and decided he qualified, a middle-aged woman entered the lounge. She reminded him of his maternal aunt – round-faced, faded, slightly overweight, dressed for comfort, and hesitant.

'You wanted to speak to me?' She screwed up her eyes, suggesting she should have worn glasses.

'That's right, Mrs Tait.'

'I can't think why.'

'There's no call to worry,' he said cheerfully.

They sat on opposite sides of a small table which bore many scars of use.

'It's like this, Mrs Tait. We've had a request from Spain asking for the address of a Mrs Tait who used to live in Southfields. Would that be you?'

'I did live there until I moved here.'

'At number sixteen, Cawdor Road.'

'Yes. But who wants to know where I am?'

'I'm afraid I can't answer that. We get the request, but usually don't get filled in for the reason.'

'You said Spain?'

'Majorca, actually. A place by the sea called Llueso. Do you know it?'

132

'I've never been to Majorca and I certainly don't know anyone there unless . . . Do you think . . . ?'

'Do I think what?'

'Could it be Bernie?'

'I'm sorry?'

'My husband. Has something happened to him?'

'Can't be anything like that, Mrs Tait, or the message we had would have said to tell you to get in touch with him.'

'Then if he's not ill . . . It must be that he wants to come back, but doesn't know where I am.'

She spoke so hopefully that he hadn't the heart to point out that it was not part of the police's duties to help husbands and wives find each other.

'When he said he was leaving me, I told him he'd come back.'

There was a sense of triumph as well as hope in her voice. Perhaps even she did not know which emotion was the stronger. 'I'll tell Spain you're living here until you move into your new house.' He stood, feeling sorry for her, whatever the reason for his inquiry, because he thought it unlikely her husband would return to someone so grey after enjoying an island of vivid colours.

When he stepped outside, it was to discover that a drizzle had begun. Bloody climate!

The ringing awoke Alvarez and he struggled into an upright position, reached out for the receiver and put it to his ear.

'Is that Inspector Alvarez? My name's Police Constable Gill, county constabulary. Do you speak English?'

'I do, yes.'

'Thank God for that! . . . How's the weather with you?'

'Too hot.'

'I suppose the beaches are packed?'

'I should imagine so.'

'It's raining here and everyone's as cheerful as a

133

drowned puppy . . . I've the good lady's address and telephone number.'

'Then you have worked a miracle!'

'You wouldn't like to tell the sergeant that, would you? His only comment was that the search took me twice as long as it should.'

'Superiors are the same the world over; incapable of appreciating initiative.'

'I like that! . . . Here's the address and number.' He gave them. 'By the way, I don't know what your angle is, but I thought you might like to hear how I found Mrs Tait?'

'I was about to ask.'

'Not very sure of herself, uncertain about life in general, and probably very fond of chintz curtains. She jumped to the conclusion that the inquiry was started by her husband who was eager to return home. Obviously she'll have him, but my money says she'll make him pay for his desertion.'

'Are you saying she's still married to him?'

'That's the way she was talking.'

'Very interesting!'

'How come?'

'He's engaged to be married to a lady here; a very wealthy lady.'

'Busy man; sensible man.'

After Gill had expressed a wish that he were out on the island enjoying the sun, sea, sand, and you-know-what, the conversation finished.

Alvarez stared into space. Salas had ordered him to have nothing more to do with the case. But there was no way in which Salas could ever find out he had made a call to Señora Tait . . .

When the connection was made, there was a wait of a couple of minutes before she came to the phone. He introduced himself. 'I am ringing from Mallorca . . .'

'It's because of my husband, isn't it?'

'Indirectly, yes.'

'He is on the island?'

'That is so. Señora, are you still married to him?'

134

'Of course I am.'

'You have not started divorce proceedings?'

'Certainly not. I don't believe in divorce.'

'Have you any reason to suppose that he has done so?'

'No. You're not saying you think . . .' She became silent.

'I have heard nothing to suggest he has. Señora, I have one final question. Why did the señor leave home?'

There was a long silence. 'I . . . I don't really know,' she finally answered. 'I wish I did. He talked about becoming old before he was old. I just didn't know what he meant. I tried and tried to understand him.'

That newly invented complaint, the male menopause? 'Has he ever been guilty of violence towards you?'

'Never! Of course not. How dare you suggest such a terrible thing? What's going on? Why are you asking all these horrible questions?'

She was a woman who probably had always failed to understand much of life. 'Señora, I am very sorry to have disturbed you, but it was necessary to ask.'

'But why?'

'In order to establish certain facts.'

'What facts?'

'I wish I were permitted to answer, but I am not.'

'Is he in some sort of trouble?'

'He is not known to be.'

'Why did you ask if he'd ever hit me?'

'I was hoping to establish that he had never done such a thing.'

'Oh! . . . Have you told him my address?'

'Not yet.'

'When you do, say I'm buying a house that looks out over fields. He's always liked the country.'

'I will not forget that.'

He said goodbye, rang off. There were evasions, half-truths, lies, and a policeman's word. He felt sufficiently contemptuous of himself to need a drink. After pouring a large one, he lit a cigarette. Halfway through the brandy, he decided that perhaps he was being irrational to confuse work and morals; by the time the glass was empty, he was convinced of that.

Tait might not have been proved to be a violent man, but he had been exposed as a potential bigamist. When a man was ready to commit one crime, he could contemplate a second one, even if it called for the use of violence, much more easily. Yet even if it was now clear that Tait had both the character and motive to have murdered Beatriz Ruig, had visited her house very shortly before her death, it seemed that the facts proved he had not murdered her because she could not have been murdered. Yet every fibre of Alvarez's instinct told him that she had not been on her own when she'd died. How to reconcile the irreconcilable, prove possible the impossible? He closed his eyes the better to concentrate and just as his mind began to hover in that peaceful emptiness which lay between being awake and being asleep, he realized that he – and even the brilliant Inspector Garicano – had missed one vital point. It was easier to break out than to break in.

The house was large and, except for the bedroom, open to any intruder. The murderer had entered, unseen and unheard, made his way up to her bedroom and there hidden in the large wardrobe. Later, she had gone upstairs and locked herself in the bedroom, undressed and changed into her nightdress. He had left the wardrobe, intent on murdering her. Fate, with the irony it so liked, had decided she should die from shock before she died from his violence.

It was natural to believe that a locked door meant no one had entered or left by it, but as every policeman knew, if secured only by the lock this was not necessarily so. When the key was on the inside, it could sometimes be turned from the outside by using an ouistiti – a pair of specially made, very thin but strong pliers; when the ouistiti would not work, a small piece of wood – a pencil, for instance – could be inserted in the handle of the key, a loop of string taken under the door which was then shut, and by careful pressure on the string the wood could be induced to turn the key after which the string was withdrawn, dropping the wood on to the floor where it was unlikely to be thought of any consequence; chain locks could be bypassed with a thumbtack, rubber band, and pencil . . . But he'd never heard of any way of sliding home bolts from the outside. So the murderer had not left by the door. The window shutters had been secured by the locking-bar. Somehow, that bar had been dropped into position from the outside, using a similar method by which one could turn a door key . . .

He remembered Salas's words. But if he could finally prove that Beatriz Ruig had been murdered, even Salas at his most irrational would have to admit that he was right to have ignored the prohibition and continued the investigation.

CHAPTER 21

Alvarez braked the car to a halt in front of Son Abrut, but did not immediately climb out as yet again he ran through the facts in his mind, trying to convince himself he had to be right. There was the snuffed-out candle, the mobile telephone, and three men each of whom had a motive for murder and either no or a very weak alibi. Motive had been called the sharpest of signposts. Yet obviously that wasn't always true. Unless Mason, Tait, and Sale had been conspiring together to murder, the motives of two of them were irrelevant. So why should that of the third not have been likewise? Without motive, proof that she had been murdered became thin indeed. Yet he 'knew' she had died from fear because one of them had intended to murder her . . .

He finally left the car, crossed to the front door, stepped inside and called out. Amelia, a duster in one hand and wearing a tattered apron over an even dowdier frock than she had been wearing the last time, appeared in the doorway of the study.

'I've come for another look at the bedroom,' he explained, after the customary greetings.

Because she had learned that he was genuinely friendly, she was emboldened to say: 'Haven't you seen enough of it by now?'

'I'm missing something.'

She said, indignantly: 'None of us has taken anything.'

'You think I don't know that if there were a million pesetas lying around, not a single one would go missing in a year? What I've been missing is the evidence that'll say how, after the señorita died, someone managed to leave behind him a locked and bolted door and fastened shutter.'

'It's impossible.'

'Perhaps not, if one uses a little ingenuity.'

She shook her head.

He climbed the stairs, unsurprised when she followed. Later, she would enjoy telling her listeners everything he had said and done; since the outside world did not press in on them through television, radio, and newspapers, the interests of all who lived in the valley were turned inwards.

He came to a stop in the middle of the sala and said, as he stared at the shattered bedroom door which had not been moved: 'Tell me everything once again. You were the first to come up here that morning?'

'I was worried. I mean, the señorita wasn't young any more and she'd had a nasty cough.'

'You knocked on the door and called out?'

'When there wasn't no answer, I shouted to Lucía.'

'You tried the door?'

'It was locked.'

'And then?'

'We called Frederico. He and Pedro broke the door down.'

'The bolts of the door were definitely shot home?'

'Can't you see?'

It was obvious from the way in which both base plates had been buckled and the screws had been partially wrenched out of the wood that the bolts must have been fast. So it was confirmed – not that this point had really needed confirmation – that the intruder had not left by the doorway.

He entered the bedroom, carefully went over to the window and visually examined the closed shutters. The bright sunshine beyond highlighted the cracks in the wood and the gaps between them and around their edges. There was, he judged, just enough room between the top of

139

either of the shutters and the stonework to thread string through the gap. Now to prove that. He went to lift the locking-bar and once again was surprised to discover how much force this required. He opened the shutters. The wall was three-quarters of a metre thick, thus providing a space in which a man could kneel as he worked the string to lower the locking-bar into position.

He took a length of thin, strong string from his trouser pocket, then awkwardly clambered backwards on to the sill, trying and not wholly succeeding to close his mind to the fact that his feet were now sticking out into space . . . Space which seemed to suck at him . . .

'Are you all right?' she asked.

Her words broke the spell. He reminded himself that the drop to the ground was no more than a few metres and surely could not prove fatal even to a coward? 'It's just the heat.'

'Never stops, does it?' she said, with the placid acceptance with which the peasant met every twist and turn of nature.

'Will you hand me the bar?'

She passed it to him. He wound the string twice around the middle, closed the shutters until they were no more than fifteen centimetres apart and he could just ease the bar between them and site it above the L-shaped holding brackets, brought the two ends of string over the top of the right-hand shutter. He pulled the shutters to and discovered that he'd chosen to position the string where it was nipped between shutter and stone. He opened the shutters until he could move the string along, closed them, found the same thing happening again. Silently swearing, he tried a third time and now the string could move reasonably freely. He released the string. When he pushed the shutters, they swung open and the locking-bar fell to the ground. This time, he swore aloud.

He scrambled back into the room with the greatest difficulty, to find Amelia was watching him with wide-eyed curiosity. He picked up the locking-bar, shut the shutters, rested the bar on the brackets; it was obvious that these were set a fraction closer to the shutters than its width (he should have realized this from the fact that the bar had taken more force to lift out than he'd expected). So the bar had to be forced into place and the string method of securing the shutters from the outside could never work.

He climbed back on to the sill and asked her to close the shutters and rest the bar on top of the brackets. He brought his penknife from his pocket and opened the small blade. If there were room between the shutters to insert this . . . Even at its widest – below the brackets – the gap was too narrow to allow the blade through.

He returned to the bedroom.

'What are you doing?' she asked.

'Proving that the impossible is impossible.'

'Sounds a daft sort of thing to do.'

He wasn't going to argue with that. Yet these days, there were surely metals made that could be drawn to a thinness of a razor blade, but possess the strength to force the locking-bar home? The murderer must have equipped himself with a length of such metal . . . Once the shutters were fastened on the inside, the murderer had had to descend from the window. To jump when the ground was bone dry must be to risk injury even though the distance was not great (a different conclusion from the one of which he had tried to convince himself earlier). The murderer had probably used a ladder. 'I imagine there's a ladder somewhere around the place?'

'There ain't.'

He had forgotten the condition of the house; no repairs had been carried out for many years and so there had been no need for one. 'You'll use 'em to harvest the almonds, algarrobas, oranges and lemons, though?'

'There are some down in the barns.'

The murderer must have collected one of those and brought it up to the house by car . . . 'Where will I find Alberto?'

141

'Could be anywhere. Up in the mountains, like as not. Sometimes he's there all day long; counting goats, so he says. Poor lad.'

He led the way downstairs, thanked her for her help, and went outside. He crossed to a point below Beatriz Ruig's bedroom window. He had not really expected to find the marks of a ladder since the ground was so hard; for the first time in quite a while, his expectations proved to be justified.

He drove slowly along the dirt track. A wise man learns, a fool yearns. He had learned that Beatriz Ruig must have been on her own at the time of death; yet he yearned to prove that she had not been. How could the murderer have known he would need a strip of metal flexible enough and thin enough to be eased between the closed shutters, yet strong enough to force down the locking-bar? She would never have allowed Tait or Sale into her bedroom and it was almost as unlikely that she would have admitted Mason . . .

Garicano was an insufferable know-all from the Peninsula, but unfortunately that didn't prevent his sometimes being right. Investigation had shown that Mason, Tait, and Sale was each a rotter in his own style, but being a rotter did not necessarily mean one was capable of murder . . . By ignoring Salas's original order to do no more than conduct a general search of the house, he had wasted endless hours and proved himself incapable of obeying orders; by allowing his judgement to be swayed by matters wholly extraneous, he had exposed the level of his incompetence. *Mea maxima culpa* . . . But it was never too late to plough a straighter furrow. From now on, he would carry out orders as if they were written on tablets of stone; ignore his instincts; judge on facts, not fantasies . . .

But just before he turned over a new leaf . . . He braked to a halt when he saw Ferrer in the company of two women who were laughing immoderately, suggesting all three were indulging in the broadest of Mallorquin humour. 'Can you spare a moment?' he called out.

Ferrer made one last comment which caused the women to laugh afresh, then trudged across, stopping briefly on his way to pick a pea pod. When he came up to the car, he split the pod with calloused thumb and rolled the peas into his mouth.

'I'd like a word with Alberto; d'you know where he is?'

'Last time I saw him, he was rebuilding a wall.'

'He's good at that kind of work?'

'Show him a pile of rock and he knows immediately what's going to fit. He'll have a couple of metres built whilst the likes of you and me is still making a mess of the footings.'

'He can be a useful bloke, then?'

'If he sticks at the job, which ain't often.'

'Whereabouts is this wall he's been working on?'

'Back of the houses.'

'I'll see if I can find him.'

'You'll need me there if he's not to run.' Ferrer opened the passenger door and went to sit down, knocked his hat off his head. He reached down and picked it up, finally settled. 'Sometimes Alberto talks sense, sometimes he don't. Best remember that.'

They reached the huddle of buildings and parked. Ferrer led the way to his patio, motioned to Alvarez to sit, went into the house and brought out a jug of wine, two mugs, and some olives. He walked out of sight beyond the next house and shouted: 'Alberto! Alberto!' When he returned, he sat, filled the mugs. 'Tomatoes is down. Fifteen pesetas the kilo.'

'They're sixty and seventy in the shops.'

'It's always them bastards make the money . . . Been meaning to ask. What happens to the señorita's share of what we sell?'

'It'll go to her heir.'

'Who's that?'

'Her nephew.'

'Think he'll live in the valley? He ain't all Mallorquin and no more is he a farmer. Don't think he'll sell, do you?'

'It's hard to know,' replied Alvarez, unwilling to tell the probable truth.

'There ain't nowhere else can grow like here.'

'Sadly, that doesn't count for much these days.'

'Don't seem right.'

'I don't suppose change ever does.'

'It were better before.'

'Some things certainly were.'

'All things were when Don Gaspar was alive.'

Yet it was he who had first neglected the valley and probably he who was responsible for his daughter's becoming a miser. If only one could live in the past of one's memory.

Pujol, closely accompanied by his dog, sidled round the corner of the house, ready to take flight at the first alarm.

'Get a mug,' Ferrer said.

Pujol, giving the table a wide berth, went into the house; the dog waited outside. When he returned, he showed none of his previous nervousness, sat on the remaining chair, smiled vacantly at Alvarez, pushed his mug across.

'The inspector wants to ask you something,' Ferrer said, as he filled the mug.

Pujol crammed several olives into his mouth and chewed, spitting out stones from time to time.

'Do you remember telling me about a car you saw driving up to the big house the night Doña Beatriz died?' Alvarez asked.

He might not have heard.

'You said it was around dusk.'

He drank noisily.

'Was there anything unusual about that car?'

He frowned, shifted uneasily on the chair.

'There's no call to be worried,' Ferrer said soothingly.

'Did the car look odd in any way?'

Pujol shook his head.

'You didn't see anything unusual on its roof?'

He shook his head again.

'What d'you expect he saw?' Ferrer asked.

'There might have been a ladder.'

'There weren't no ladder.' Pujol spoke with such emphasis it was as though someone had just been arguing with him.

Alvarez turned to Ferrer. 'Amelia said you've some ladders down here?'

'Need 'em for the harvests, don't we?'

'Could someone have picked up one that night without any of you knowing?'

'If anyone had gone looking in the barns, the dogs would have given tongue.'

Confirmation that his previous theory had been nonsense; that Garicano had been correct; that he should have kept his promise to himself, made only minutes before he'd broken it.

'You're going to show me the goats,' Pujol said suddenly.

He'd completely forgotten his promise. Which showed that he was not only a lousy detective, but also that he had a lousy memory. 'I'll take you as soon as I have the time.' He drank deeply. The greatest gift of wine was that it gave a man reason to continue to live with himself.

CHAPTER 22

Over the phone, the laboratory assistant said: 'About those documents you sent us.'

Alvarez struggled to remember what they were.

'It is highly probable that the signature on the contract is a forgery, but due to the fact that there is only one control signature and this does vary in detail from the specimen – probably because the writer is old and all her signatures have become erratic – it is not possible to be definite. Sorry about that, but it's the best we can do. There's one more thing. The date on the contract was written with the same pen and ink as the specimen.'

He settled back. So Tait was the forger that he had judged him to be – though this could not be proved in court with the evidence to hand. Tait could only have needed to forge Beatriz Ruig's signature because she had refused to sign the contract; he would only have dared commit the forgery if he had judged it would never be brought to light. If he had murdered her, he would have known she could never challenge it. Yet that didn't prove he had been responsible for her death because it was equally logical to believe he had committed the forgery only after he had learned of her death . . .

He swore. He was becoming stupider by the hour. Since he had proved there could have been no one else in the bedroom when she died, it was the height of nonsense to query whether this forgery did, or did not, prove that Tait had been.

In a burst of ambitious enthusiasm, he decided to prove to the world, and to himself, that he was a far more

146

responsible detective than the past might suggest. He would start by organizing himself. He collected together the mass of unopened letters, internal memoranda, and general paperwork, which had accumulated and began to sort it . . .

It was undeniably a boring task. He checked the time and was disheartened to find that there was still an hour before the earliest moment at which he could break off work and return home. His mind drifted. Dolores had been in such a good mood recently that it was possible she was cooking one of her more memorable meals. What could that be? His imagination ranged far and wide . . .

The telephone interrupted his gastronomic dreams. He reached across the pile of papers and lifted the receiver.

'This is Dr Casanovas. I understand that you are conducting inquiries into the death of Señorita Ruig?'

'That's right, Doctor. Inspector Garicano was involved in a car accident soon after he began his investigation and has been off work since then.'

'Very well. I think you should know that there has been a second death in the valley. A man called Ferrer.'

Ferrer! The poor old man. 'Sweet Mary, but that's sad news.'

'He had a long life,' said the doctor with professional realism.

'The nature of his death is suspicious?'

'There is no reason to suppose it anything other than an accident. However, when one of the women said you were still investigating the señorita's death, I decided you should be informed of this.'

'Do you know what happened?'

'He was part way up a mountain when he slipped and fell over what is virtually a sheer drop. Since he landed on his head, death will have been instantaneous. I can tell you no more than that. Incidentally, I have given strict orders that the body is not to be touched until you give authority for this.'

147

'Thanks . . . I'll have a word with the Institute of Forensic Anatomy and then drive over to the valley.'

After the conclusion of that call, Alvarez spoke to Professor Fortunata's secretary. When he replaced the receiver, he began to drum on the desk with his fingers. Coincidences happened all the time and there was some reason for saying that the more unlikely they seemed, the more likely to be genuine. Yet for a second unusual death to occur within fifteen days of the first was asking rather a lot of coincidences. Especially when one remembered that the favourite method of concealing a murder was to make it look like an accident . . . Ferrer had known something which would have named the señorita's death murder and have helped identify the murderer, but had not realized he did; or he must have mentioned it, since between him – as for every other villager – and the señorita there had existed not only the relationship of landowner and landworker, but a primitive sense of devotion that was the product of centuries and which demanded she be avenged. What could that something have been? Which of the three men had it incriminated?

Death was no stranger to Alvarez, yet familiarity with it failed to lessen his fear of the lesson that it taught – all men were mortal.

In death, Ferrer was no more than a shattered huddle of old age. There remained no hint of the character which had earned, not demanded, respect; of the strength which had enabled him to overcome the pain of life; of his generosity of spirit which had led him to befriend a simple youth who had been rejected by his own father.

'Can we move him?' asked one of the two tearful women who guarded his body from blowflies with rough straw swats.

'Not until the doctor has come from Palma.'

They resumed their vigil. Both already had black shawls. As soon as possible, they would be in black from head to foot.

He turned and looked at the fountain, which maintained its unvarying rhythm a dozen metres to his left, as oblivious to tragedy as to joy, then up at the mountain. At the point from which Ferrer had fallen, the face was virtually sheer. Above, the slope was steep, but not precipitous and partially covered in clumps of weed grass, cistus, brambles, and rosebay willowherb.

There was the sound of pounding feet and Pujol ran up, his expression wild, his hands cleaving the air in outlandish gestures. He came to a stop in front of the body and as tears welled out of his eyes and rolled down his cheeks, he began to shout, at first incoherently, then the words became just understandable. 'It's not true. It's not true. It can't be true.'

One of the women put a hand out to comfort him. He dashed it away with sufficient force to make her gasp, turned, ran off, shouting.

'Frederico was a father to him,' she said.

'Yes, I know,' Alvarez replied.

'It'll take him time to get over it.'

'An age.' Could anyone, of whatever state of mind, ever come to terms with such uncomprehending grief?

He was certain he couldn't do it, yet knew he had to. He was so terrified that already he had started panic-sweating and his stomach churned . . . He forced himself to move, when every last atom of his mind demanded he stayed. Thirty metres beyond the sheer face, the slope was sufficiently relaxed for him to start climbing. A mountaineer would have bounded up; he moved centimetre by centimetre, dreading the missed foothold, the falling rock, the attack of acute giddiness, that would send him crashing down to a nightmare death. Yet even as he experienced the depths of fear, he suffered the desire to search out that fatal fall . . .

It was worse above the sheer face. Here, there was only space. The call of the sirens became louder. The brave man died once; the coward a thousand times . . .

There was no broken branch of a cistus bush, no

recently flattened grass, no disarranged trail of bramble, no broken stalk of willowherb; there were pockets of crumbled stone or poor soil, it was difficult to tell which, but in none was there any mark of human passage; there was nothing to suggest that Ferrer had ever walked there, slipped, and fallen into the void. But on such a surface, the negative could never become a positive. The lack of any trace did not mean he probably had not been there. The only valid conclusion was the question, Why should he have been there?

It was impossible, but descent was even more horrifying than the ascent. His body was plucked by unseen forces, his mind by terrifying desires . . . On reaching the ground, he collapsed to sit on a round-topped rock. With hand shaking badly, he lit a cigarette. He would have given a fortune for a brandy; half a fortune for a mug of Ferrer's harsh wine.

It was half an hour later when a car drove up to come to a stop behind the Ibiza. A youngish, tall, thin man climbed out, cupped his hands about his mouth and shouted: 'Inspector!'

Alvarez walked to the road.

'I'm Dr Minguez.' He shook hands. 'The professor's tied up and couldn't come out, so he sent me.' His manner was pleasant, but brisk. 'What's the situation?'

'I can't tell you very much, I'm afraid, because so far I've only had the chance to speak to the two women there, watching over the body, and they're too distressed to make much sense. But as far as I've been able to make out, a man came across to alter the flow of water in one of the main irrigation channels and saw the body. Dr Casanovas was called and after confirming Ferrer was dead – sadly, not difficult – he telephoned me. He remarked that there was nothing to suggest that Ferrer had not accidentally fallen, but that in view of the circumstances of Señorita Ruig's death fifteen days ago, an investigation might be necessary.'

'And you have reached a conclusion as to that?'

'No, I haven't . . . I would not say this to the superior chief, Doctor, but I do have the instinctive feeling that there is a direct connection between the two deaths.'

Minguez turned and opened the front car door, brought out a small, battered leather case. He followed Alvarez across to where the body lay. The two women backed away and as Minguez began his examination, wailed, the intonation Moorish in origin.

Minguez was a quick, thorough worker, yet it was almost three-quarters of an hour before he stripped off surgical gloves and dropped them into a plastic bag. He produced a pack of Marlboro cigarettes, offered it, flicked open a lighter. 'Rigor's just begun and is present in face and jaw. That and the drop in body temperature suggest, subject to the usual proviso, that he died between five and seven hours ago.'

Alvarez looked at his wristwatch. 'That means at or soon after daybreak.'

'The injuries are fully conversant with his landing head first from a considerable height and there are embedded fragments of rock and dirt. There is heavy bruising almost certainly caused as momentum carried the body forwards and sideways after striking the ground. While there are no other external injuries, obviously had there been any to the head before the fall, evidence of these would have been obscured. So far, everything is consistent with his falling from a considerable height, despite the minor degree of ground-staining; the extent of this can be strangely capricious. However, you were right when you said it might not have been an accident. There is clear evidence that the body was moved after death. Are you conversant with the term, lividity?'

'Only in very general terms.'

'Then to be a little more specific. It is the staining of the skin, as well as dependent parts, which results from passive distension by blood; it starts within a couple of hours of death and is marked in five or six hours. Since the stains cannot develop where there is pressure – for

151

instance, where the buttocks are pressed against the ground – their absence as much as their presence can provide a good guide to whether the body has been moved. The dead man was lying with both buttocks against rock, yet there are signs of lividity on the right-hand one.'

Alvarez drew on the cigarette. Ferrer had been murdered somewhere else and then brought to the fountain to make it appear his death had resulted from an accidental fall.

CHAPTER 23

As he stood immediately outside Son Abrut and spoke to Salas over the mobile phone, Alvarez had quite a task to keep his tone respectful rather than triumphant. Near the end of his report, he became less successful. 'So obviously the murder of Ferrer is directly related to the death of the señorita; in which case, her death was almost certainly caused by terror which in turn means that there was someone in her bedroom . . .'

'That was always a possibility,' cut in Salas.

'But . . . but when I suggested that, señor, you said . . .'

'I said you were to keep the possibility firmly in mind. Unfortunately, but perhaps not surprisingly, you clearly failed to do so.'

'Señor, you very distinctly told me . . .'

'Just for once, Alvarez, don't argue. Which of the three suspects does not have an alibi for the time of death of Ferrer?'

'I can't say since I have only just . . .'

'Is the evidence of the villagers of any account?'

'I haven't yet had time to question them . . .'

'An efficient officer, if you can understand the term, makes time. Have you taken any steps at all to commence investigations into this latest murder?'

'I have told the villagers I'll need to question them . . .'

'Then I suggest you start doing so instead of wasting both our times.'

'Señor, to pursue my investigations further, I will need details of Señor Sale's bank accounts. May I have your authority to make the necessary request?'

153

'Why not follow your usual course and falsely assume you have it?' snapped Salas, before he cut the connection.

'Just tell me what happened?' Alvarez said.

Pedro Estranay looked at his wife, who stood to the right of the soot-blackened open fireplace, then down at the concrete floor of the small kitchen. 'I was working.'

'Where?'

'In the fields.'

'Whereabouts in the fields?'

'Where we're planting peppers.'

'Is that near the estanque?'

'Not so far away.'

As well as he understood the Mallorquin peasant, Alvarez could not decide whether Estranay was the unintelligent, sullen man he now appeared to be or was merely exhibiting to a greater degree than usual the typical reaction to authority. 'So you walked towards the estanque. Why?'

'Why d'you think?'

'Tell me.'

'Needed more water in the channel, that's why.'

'And you saw him as you approached the estanque?'

'He was lying there.'

'Did you examine him to see if he was dead?'

'When his head was like a squashed melon?'

Estranay's wife began to wail. He roughly ordered her to shut up.

'What did you do next?'

'Told the others.'

'And then?'

'Told José to get the doctor.'

'From the moment you left this house to start work, did you see anyone or anything unusual?'

'How d'you mean?'

'Was there anyone on the mountains?'

'Never saw no one.'

'Did any vehicle drive into or out of the valley?'

154

'No.'

'Did Frederico often walk in the mountains?'

He shrugged his shoulders.

'Have you seen him walking 'em before?'

'Not since we collected the snow.'

'How long ago was that?'

'When I was a young 'un.'

'Why d'you imagine he was up in the mountains very early this morning?'

'Wouldn't know.'

'Did he ever mention the señorita's death?'

Estranay's wife began to wail again; he shouted at her. 'Don't remember,' he finally muttered.

'You never heard him say how he thought she'd died?'

'Hit her head, didn't she?'

'Did you ever hear him mention the name Mason, or Tait, or Sale?'

'No.'

'Did he ever talk about an Englishman without actually naming him?'

The question confused Estranay. When it had been simplified and he understood it, he said he'd never heard Ferrer talk about any Englishman.

It seemed probable – he'd spoken to many of the others – that Ferrer had never so much as hinted at any evidence which could identify the señorita's murderer. Surely that was because he'd never realized he was in possession of such evidence? Every able peasant had sharp eyes and, in certain matters, a sharp mind. So this evidence was probably apparently unconnected with the valley or he would have understood its significance and commented on it. Yet since he had had so little to do with life beyond the valley and probably visited the outside world as seldom as possible, how would he have come into possession of such evidence?

Alvarez thanked Estranay, who glowered, and left. The death of Ferrer had shocked and bewildered the villagers and they had abandoned the fields and gathered in groups about the houses, the men talking, the women crying or dumbly grieving. When Alvarez appeared, they became silent as they stared at him. It was, he thought, like being surrounded by a herd of cows which did not know whether to stay from curiosity or run. 'Is there anyone who can tell me why Frederico was walking on the mountain?' he called out.

No one answered.

'Is there anyone who was up at daybreak?'

They looked at each other, moved uneasily, remained silent.

Garicano would have cursed them for their dumb stupidity. He spoke in kind, simple words and explained why he was asking the questions. If someone had been up at daybreak to see Ferrer leave home and head for the mountains, that someone might have noticed something which would suggest his motive. Perhaps there'd been a stranger in the valley . . .

He learned that they no longer rose at daybreak – at least one thing had changed in the past hundred years! – but soon after sunrise. No one had seen Ferrer then. It might have been unusual for him not to start work with the rest of them, but no one had thought to visit his house to find out if he'd been taken ill. There had been neither a stranger nor a strange car in the valley throughout the morning. Estranay had been the first to approach the estanque.

Alvarez left, watched without hostility as he climbed into his car and drove off.

Ferrer had been murdered, he thought, at around daybreak. How had someone reached his house without the dogs barking an alarm? At least that was one question which could be easily answered. Mallorquin dogs spent all day and most of the night barking with the consequence that no notice was taken of them; most of the time, the listeners didn't even 'hear' them. What had been used to entice Ferrer up into the mountains? Money? Threats? Promises?

There was one small restaurant in Escalla. Despite the fact that it was after four, they agreed to serve him lunch. It was not really their fault, he mournfully tried to convince himself as he chewed a piece of unusually tough meat, that the meal was only a thin shadow of the one Dolores would have served a couple of hours previously.

Tait opened the door of his flat. 'The bad penny suffers from lumbago compared to you!' he said jovially. 'But if you've come with more questions, I'm afraid that this time they'll have to wait. I'm on my way out.'

'Are you visiting Señora Owen?' Alvarez asked.

'Who I'm visiting is classified information. So if you don't mind, I'm just going to have to say goodbye.'

'Señor, I can speak to you here, when what you say will be between just the two of us; or it can be at the señora's house when she will naturally hear everything.'

Tait's expression became watchful. 'You're suggesting I could have anything to say I wouldn't want her to hear?' His tone had remained jovial.

'It is very likely.'

'You intrigue me! Very well, I'll give you five minutes.' He spoke as if he were granting a favour.

They went through to the sitting-room and sat. 'Now, what is so indelicate as not to be whispered in mixed company?'

'I have received the report on the señorita's signature. It is a forgery. You forged it because you knew she was dead.'

'I have never forged anything, not even a parent's letter to school excusing my absence. That signature was genuine. I suppose your people have made the mistake because the old girl wrote so seldom that her signature must have varied tremendously.'

Alvarez admired Tait's quick thinking.

'If you reckon my fiancée would have been shocked beyond reason by that . . .'

'There is something else.'

157

'More substantial?'

'I suppose that depends on one's judgement. And on one's standards. Would the señora think it of substantial interest to learn that while you are engaged to her, you are still married to your wife?'

Tait looked away so that his face was half hidden. He moistened his lips, went to speak, checked himself. Finally, he said, as confidently as possible: 'I was married, true; very happily, until Hannah went to needlework classes. She'd always been keen on that sort of thing, so I never thought twice about it. That is, up until the day she told me she was leaving to live with the woman who was teaching. That hurt! Christ, how it hurt! There's the pain of separation and, on top of that, the certainty that people are sniggering. There was no trouble over the divorce, of course, not with such clear-cut evidence. When it was over, all I wanted to do was to get as far away as possible . . .

'I really do have to thank you for your discretion in making certain Mabel didn't have to hear all this. I suppose some people would say I ought to tell her. But if I did, she might start to think that the break-up with Hannah was due to some inadequacy on my part. It wasn't . . . Mabel and I are so fond of each other that I'd hate anything to happen that could cast the slightest cloud.'

'Such feelings do you credit.'

'Thank you.'

'So it is a pity that they are false.'

'Look, I've told you . . .'

'Enough lies to make you a politician. It was you who left home, not she. There has been no divorce.'

'Who says there hasn't?'

'Your wife.'

After a moment, Tait said: 'You've talked to her?'

'Over the telephone. Which reminds me that she asked me to give you a message. She'll forgive you.'

'She would, the —' He stopped abruptly. Then he said: 'It's easy to criticize when you only know one side.

158

Suppose you listen to what it was like for me? She was middle aged when she was still in her twenties; middle aged and reluctant. Animals got cracking because they were animals, civilized people did the crossword instead. It was like being married to a pensioned nun.'

'Your private life does not interest me, your public one does. What really happened at Son Abrut on the night the señorita was murdered?'

'I've told you a dozen times.'

'You have lied a dozen times. It was your car in the valley at dusk.'

'It was parked outside my fiancée's house all evening.'

'Would it not be better to tell me the truth now rather than when the señora will be listening? It must be in your interests she should not learn the truth since you would not wish her to understand you were swindling her by using a proposal of marriage as the security for the loan of money to buy the valley.'

'You . . . You're blackmailing me!' Tait said, his voice expressing shock. 'If this were England . . .'

'But it is Mallorca. And on the island sympathies lie with the victim and not with the criminal.'

'You can't prove a bloody thing.'

'It will be Señora Owen who will wish to do that, by speaking to Señora Tait.'

'The truth will be what I tell my wife it is.'

'Perhaps you could persuade her by using false promises to support your lies. But I wonder how you will manage to get in touch with her?'

'How d'you think? By phone.'

'But phoning where? She has sold the house in Southfields and moved.'

'You're bluffing.'

'Call my bluff. Ring Cawdor Road. You will find that Señora Prescot now lives there and she does not know where your wife has moved to.'

Tait did not move; the silence lasted until he finally said: 'What do you want?'

159

'The truth. It was your car which drove up to Son Abrut, wasn't it?'

'Yes.'

'And you went there to try to persuade her to sign the contract?'

'Yes.'

'But she refused because she'd learned you were swindling her out of a million dollars?'

'It's not swindling when you buy something more cheaply than you can sell it.'

'Our definitions differ. Her refusal must have made you very angry?'

'You can't expect it to have made me laugh.'

'So angry that you threatened her with violence?'

'No, I bloody well didn't. Maybe I've sailed close to the line, but I've never done anything like that.'

'A very large financial loss can make even a peaceable man violent.'

'I argued and argued, I offered her more only she wouldn't listen. The thought of two million had turned her crazy.'

'What did you do when you couldn't get her to sign the contract?'

'Left.'

'You were prepared to lose a million dollars without a fight?'

'I reckoned that in a day or two I'd be able to make her understand why it had to be much better for her if she sold through me.'

'Where did you leave her?'

'In the study.'

'Was she dressed?'

'D'you think she'd walk around starkers?'

'When did you forge her signature?'

'You can't prove I did.'

'That was not my question.'

'If I had, it would have been as soon as I heard she was dead. But I didn't.'

160

'Where were you at daybreak this morning?'

'What's that?'

Alvarez repeated the question.

Tait suspiciously studied the question before answering: 'In bed.'

'On your own?'

'Mabel's very old-fashioned. Besides, she has Bobby.'

'There is no one who can vouch you were in this flat?'

'What's it matter where I was?'

'There has been another murder in the valley.'

'Who?'

'Frederico Ferrer.'

'Who's he?'

'One of the men who works the land.'

'Never met him. And if you're crazy enough to think I croaked him, I've just said, I can't stand violence.'

'You restrict yourself to forgery and fraud?' said Alvarez with contempt as he stood.

CHAPTER 24

In the summer, the banks closed on Saturdays. It was said that this was because of the increased demand for their services due to the tremendous influx of tourists. It was a logic more readily understood by the Latin than the Anglo-Saxon mind. It was not until Monday that Alvarez was able to speak on the phone to the manager of the Pietro branch of Sa Nostra.

'I have the details of the account in front of me – what exactly is it you want to know?'

'Whether in the past year, Señor Sale has paid in a very considerable sum and if so, what happened to it.'

'The first answer is easily given. In January, four million and forty thousand pesetas were paid into his account in cash. But to follow that money through will be extremely time-consuming and difficult, perhaps impossible.'

'Were any large sums paid out very shortly afterwards?'

'One million pesetas were withdrawn the next day. Following that, there were several withdrawals of fifty thousand or more.'

'This first sum – how much was it for and can you say to whom it went?'

'A million pesetas, transferred to the mortgage account.'

'What mortgage account?'

'Señor Sale was granted a mortgage to buy his flat some time ago and, strictly between you and me, he'd fallen badly behind in making repayments. In fact, at the beginning of January we had to issue a warning that if he didn't clear the account to date, we'd have to repossess. The million covered all interest due and paid off a part of the capital.'

This time, Sale's wife did not suggest she had to leave the flat to minister to the sick and elderly. She sat with her husband on the settee and as he struggled to answer the questions, she gripped his hand, trying to impart strength as well as sympathy.

'Four million and forty thousand pesetas is a considerable sum even today,' Alvarez said.

'Values are always relative,' Sale replied. 'And if one's used to dealing in millions of pounds and dollars . . .'

'At a time when you had not been able to meet the mortgage repayments and interest due, that sum would have seemed a positive fortune.'

'Who says I couldn't handle the mortgage?'

'The bank who granted it.'

'Oh! . . . Well, there was a little temporary difficulty.'

'The problem had been there for a long time. Repossession was threatened in January and that was after many months of default.'

'The bank had no right to tell you my private affairs.'

'They were under an obligation to do so.'

'Then it's still a bloody dictatorship.'

She whispered something.

'You stole Señorita Ruig's money,' Alvarez said. 'And also perhaps all the smaller sums of money you paid out the following week.'

'That's utter nonsense.'

'She gave it to you to invest on her behalf, but you used at least part of it for your own purposes. That is theft.'

'I . . . I did borrow a little of it.'

'With her knowledge and assent?'

'Of course.'

'You have proof of that?'

'We trusted each other.'

'Her trust was badly misplaced since you couldn't even keep up the mortgage repayments.'

'I've investments that are going to come good.'

'Why did you not use them to meet the mortgage repayments and thus avoid any chance of repossession?'

'I'd have had to cash them in before they rose.'

'Will you show me proof that you hold investments in your name?'

Sale looked at his wife, but all she could do was to continue to grip his hand and to whisper encouragement. 'I . . .' He became silent.

'Señorita Ruig discovered that you'd swindled her, didn't she?'

'I've told you, it was a loan. I was going to pay the proper interest.'

'She was a miser who would never have parted with a peseta if you hadn't promised to double her savings within months. Because money meant everything to her, she watched the course of her investments with a far sharper eye than you ever imagined she possessed. So what happened? Did some of the imaginary shares, imaginatively bought with the money you'd stolen, suddenly leap so much in value that she demanded you sell them so she could revel in the profit? But as they were only in your imagination, you couldn't do that, which made her put two and two together?'

'It wasn't anything like that.'

'Then what was it like?'

'It was just that . . . Well, somehow almost all the shares in her portfolio fell, despite the general trend. She was on the phone God knows how many times, blaming me. But I couldn't control a market that was irrational.'

'So ironically it was incompetence in the choice of shares which you actually did buy that alerted her to your theft of the money of the shares you *didn't* buy! You knew that any police investigation would uncover the fact that you'd been guilty of theft, so on that Thursday you went to her house to try somehow to persuade her you were honest. When you realized you'd failed, you panicked and threatened her and terrified her to such an extent that she died from shock.'

'No!' There was a long silence. 'All right,' Tait finally said, bitterly and fearfully.

'What does that mean?'

'When I tried to explain, she did get wild, but I managed to make her calm down.'

'How?'

'I . . . I said that market sentiment had changed and the latest information was that all her shares had finally begun to rise.'

'Had they?'

'No, but I had to . . . Well . . .'

'Try anything to cover up the swindle and theft for as long as possible.'

'In the end, she agreed not to complain to anyone, so there was no way I scared her. None. D'you understand? None.'

'Very well. Let's move on. Where were you at daybreak on Friday?'

'What . . . what's the matter?' Sale asked.

'There was another murder in the valley.'

'You think . . . My God!, you're crazy.' He turned to his wife. 'He's crazy!'

She released her husband's hand in order to put her arms around him. She faced Alvarez over his shoulder. 'Can't you see what kind of a man he is? Only a fool could ever think he'd hurt someone.'

'Señora, fool or not, I must have an answer to my question.'

'He was in bed with me.'

'Have you any way of proving that?'

'You think we invite a friend in for a *ménage à trois*?'

Sale might be a murderer, he was crooked and weak, but she loved him, in part perhaps because he relied on her for strength; so no unusual relationships.

*   *   *

165

Vich said sourly: 'He claimed he'd done enough extra time to have an afternoon off.'

'To do what?'

'To take his woman on the beach. Always after her. Doesn't think of anything else.'

'Would you?'

'When I was his age, I worked.'

'Only because you weren't given an option. I want some information.'

'You lot's always wanting something.'

'D'you know the old-fashioned kind of shutters – solid and secured on the inside with a bar?'

''Course I do.'

'How would you go about closing and locking 'em fast from the outside?'

'Not being a bloody stupid detective, I wouldn't.'

'There are gaps between the shutters and the stonework and between the two inside edges when they're closed. But I reckon the widest of these is no more than roughly half a millimetre. You're on the outside and you've managed to rest the locking-bar on the L-shaped brackets, but they're set slightly closer than the width of the bar so that this doesn't drop into place but has to be pushed down with enough force to spring the brackets slightly. So I need a length of metal thin enough and flexible enough to be threaded through a gap and then strong enough that it can be used to bring sufficient pressure on the bar to force it down. Where do I find such metal?'

'How the hell would I know?'

'You've none here?'

'Never no need for it.'

'But it must be possible to obtain it from somewhere?'

Vich shrugged his shoulders.

'It might have been ordered through the garage?'

'When I do the ordering?'

Assuming that it was possible to obtain such metal, it clearly hadn't been bought through the garage. Vich would keep an eagle eye on every order, making certain he wasn't diddled out of so much as a couple of screws . . . Alvarez thanked him for his help – thanks received with sardonic contempt – and returned to his car. He started the engine, but did not drive off immediately. If he were to return home at a reasonable time – i.e., to enjoy a drink or two before the meal – he needed to leave Playa del Covetas now. But if he failed to question Mason today, he would have to return tomorrow. So it was perhaps worth it in the long run to make the short detour to where he had met Diana and Mason before, since people tended to favour the same beach. He drove off.

As he moved along the gently curving shoreline, he considered certain facts. If the murderer had left Son Abrut through the bedroom window, he must have planned the murder carefully and this called for considerable knowledge of both the house and the señorita's routine; to manipulate the locking-bar of the shutters into position and then force it home called for manual dexterity; to descend from the window to the ground in the dark demanded nerve; to return to the valley and murder Ferrer called for even greater nerve and, probably, strength. Mason was young, strong, manually dexterous and recently had frequently visited the house; Tait and Sale were middle aged, overweight, not strong, possibly fumble-fisted, had made only occasional visits, and by character were far more capable of committing a crime which involved no violence than one that called for the ultimate violence . . .

Mason's car was parked in the same spot as before and two towels and a beach bag were set out where they had sunbathed. Alvarez sat and, shielding his eyes with his hand, studied the swimmers. He identified Diana immediately. She stood, the water up to her waist, proudly bare breasted. He watched two men walk past on the sand and silently cursed them as they stared, no doubt lubriciously, at her.

She noticed him. She called out and a nearby head rose to reveal Mason. He strode through the water and up to

167

where Alvarez stood. 'What the hell d'you want now?' he demanded angrily.

'A few more answers.'

Diana reached Mason's side. 'Is something wrong?'

'Yeah. We can't have a peaceful afternoon on the beach.'

'Señorita,' said Alvarez, gallantly rising to his feet, 'I need to ask a few more questions.'

'Can't you understand, Nigel just couldn't have done anything to hurt his aunt?'

This man had gained her love. So how had he rewarded her? By screwing a couple of putas. How could perfection be so blind to such corruption? . . .

'Why are you looking like that?' She sounded almost scared.

He checked his racing thoughts. 'I am sorry, señorita, but there are times when I suffer a certain pain.'

'Oh, dear! I hope it's nothing serious?'

'It will soon go.'

Mason sat. 'So what the hell is it this time?'

Diana settled by his side, Alvarez opposite him. 'Have you heard that there has been a second death in the valley?' Alvarez asked.

'No.'

'Frederico Ferrer has been killed.'

She said shrilly: 'But you don't . . . You can't . . .'

'You think I've turned into a serial killer?' Mason asked with angry sarcasm.

'I am here to consider the possibility that you can help me.'

'You really do think I went along and knocked him on the head for the fun of it?'

'How did you know he died from head injuries?'

Mason stared at him. 'I don't know what the hell he died from. I just used that as a figure of speech.'

'An unfortunate one in the circumstances.'

'I'm not known for being lucky. But if you reckon that I killed him, you're so bloody thick . . .'

'Nigel, please be calm.'

She had pressed against him as a way of emphasizing her plea and her right breast touched his left arm. Alvarez tried not to imagine what the touch of the silken flesh was like . . . 'Did you know Ferrer?'

'I might have spoken to him without knowing his name,' Mason answered, speaking far more calmly.

'He was perhaps the oldest of the villagers and was called the headman.'

'Then I knew him. Presumably, that makes me the murderer?'

'What did you discuss with him?'

'All the things farmers are interested in. He'd no other conversation.'

'Did he ever mention another Englishman in any context?'

'No.'

'Where were you at daybreak, Friday morning?'

'Where the hell d'you think? In bed.'

'Were you on your own?'

'Yes, I was.'

Alvarez stood.

Diana looked up at him and seemed to be about to speak, then turned her head away. He walked back to his car, feeling sadder than for a very long time.

The superior chief's secretary told him in superior plum-filled tones to wait and he waited, receiver to his ear. Through the open window came the sounds of Pipes of Pan, signifying the fact that the knife grinder was ready to sharpen knives. There was a measure of pleasure to be gained from the evidence that at least one of the old customs of itinerant service had been allowed to survive . . .

'Well?'

Salas's harsh question startled him so much that it took him time to pull himself together. 'Señor, I have questioned the three suspects. Each of them claims to have

169

been sleeping at the time of Ferrer's murder; Sale with his wife, Tait and Mason on his own.'

'One of them's lying.'

'Assuredly. But which one?'

'You ask me? Do you not understand it is your task to answer that question?'

'Señor, my words were really an expression of my sense of frustration, by which I mean . . .'

'Whenever I talk to you, I am all too aware of the meaning. Why waste my time telling me you have attained nothing?'

'You told me to report to you . . .'

'When you had something concrete to report. On reflection that does, of course, suggest an unwarranted optimism.'

'It is a difficult inquiry . . .'

'With which you will no longer need to be concerned. Inspector Garicano has recovered from injuries that unfortunately, both for him and the progress of this case, proved more serious than at first thought and he will take over the investigation. Since he is not a man who gains a perverse pleasure from complicating and confusing, I expect a very quick conclusion to this case.' Salas cut the connection.

A man could only do his best.

The latest episode of the current popular soap opera, set in Brazil and dubbed into Spanish, came to an end. As the credits rolled, Dolores said: 'What a swine! How could he treat her like that?'

'What does she expect when she wouldn't come across?' As so often happened, Jaime spoke without thought.

'And for you that is all important?'

'If she . . .'

'No matter that she has spent every day, all day, slaving for him?'

'A husband has the right . . .'

'A husband has no right when he blindly, arrogantly, stupidly, and selfishly treats his wife with contempt.'

'He bought her that dress.'

'And why? Because he had a guilty conscience. Which is more than some men I know could ever suffer.'

There was a stubborn streak in Jaime's character which some might have called stupidity. Instead of accepting that he was totally in the wrong, he called out: 'Hey, Enrique, you agree with me, don't you?'

Alvarez jerked his mind back to the present. 'What's that?'

'A bloke's entitled to enjoy himself elsewhere if the wife puts up the shutters.'

'Who are you talking about?'

'Luis, of course. Where have you been?'

'I was thinking.' The moment he saw the look Dolores gave him, he knew he'd made a mistake.

'About that foreign woman, no doubt!' she snapped.

'Yes, but not in the sense you're meaning.'

'Has not my husband just informed me that a man thinks of only one thing? . . . Aiee! But has any woman ever suffered as much as I? A husband who has pickled his brains in alcohol and a cousin who dreams of women without shame instead of women with fincas of many cuarteradas.'

CHAPTER 25

To leave the parched, unproductive land and drive
through the narrow entrance into the fertile valley was
to enter an apparent Arcadia. But even as Alvarez stared
through the windscreen at the burgeoning crops, he
sighed. On earth, did there always have to be a fatal
maggot because only heaven must enjoy perfection?

He parked alongside an Alfa Romeo that was in front
of the house. He began to walk across to the front door,
came to a stop and stared up at the window of the señorita's bedroom. Exactly how had the murderer managed
to leave the shutters fast behind himself?

'What do you want?'

He looked down. Standing in the doorway was a
dapper-looking man, slightly shorter than he, dressed in
a linen suit that had been newly pressed. 'I could ask you
the same question,' he remarked politely.

'Don't try to get smart or you'll be in trouble.'

The air of superior authority and the affected accent
together provided the identification. 'You are Inspector
Garicano?'

'Yes. Who are you?'

'Enrique Alvarez.'

Garicano studied Alvarez. 'Good God!' he finally said.

'The superior chief told me you'd be returning to work.
I'm glad you're fit again.'

'Thank you.'

'He also said you'd be taking over the case immediately.
In which case, you'd like me to fill you in on the facts.'

'That won't be necessary.'

172

'But surely . . .'

'The superior chief made a point of informing me that my investigation would be more readily conducted if I relied solely on my own judgements.'

He persevered. 'There are the shutters, though. I've checked them very thoroughly and in my opinion . . .'

'I made my own examination of them before my accident.'

'Since it has to be certain that the murderer found a way of fastening them from the outside . . .'

'There was no one else in the bedroom when the old woman died and therefore no murderer.'

'But the two deaths have to be connected, which means she was murdered – or frightened to death, if you wish to be strictly accurate . . .'

'I am never anything else.'

'Yes, well, I suppose we all strive for that happy state of affairs, but sometimes it's not so easy . . .'

'Excuses are the apologia of inefficiency.'

'You don't think . . . ?'

'As I remarked to the superior chief, if one has the intelligence to maintain an open mind until all the facts are known, there can be no room for faulty logic. I have not, naturally, started with the conviction that the two deaths are connected. So I have re-examined the bedroom without suffering from any preconceptions and have been able to confirm that since it is quite impossible to secure the shutters with the locking-bar except from the inside, no one else was in the bedroom when she died. The lack of any possible connection between the two deaths immediately precludes any assumption that the old man was murdered.'

'I have never heard of a dead man who could move around.'

'Sarcasm is the wit of a sterile mind.'

'You know, it is still possible that the truth is well hidden. I think if . . .'

'As I have already said, I prefer to make my own judgements. You may accept the fact that as from eight o'clock, I have been in command of the investigation.'

'There's no way I can help?'

'Most unlikely.' Garicano turned smartly round and went inside; he pulled the door shut with unnecessary force.

Alvarez drove away, grateful he no longer had to strain his brains to uncover the truth, irritated that he had failed to discover what that was, sad that duty would not bring him back to this valley. He was almost at the entrance when he saw a shambling figure by the side of the dirt track and recognized Pujol. He slowed the car, called out. Pujol continued walking, head bowed, shuffling his feet as if they were restricted by chains. Alvarez drove ahead, stopped, climbed out of the car.

Pujol prepared to run.

'Surely you remember me, Alberto?'

He shook his head.

'We had a mug of wine more than once with Frederico.'

'He's dead.'

'Yes. It's very sad.'

Pujol began to cry.

'Try to remember that he lived to a good age. And sad as it is, in the end we all have to die.' Even as he spoke, Alvarez recognized the banality of his words.

Pujol took a couple of shuffling paces forward, suddenly said, his expression excited: 'You're taking me to see the goats!'

'When I've more . . .' Alvarez abruptly stopped. Was he not in a position to grant Pujol a brief release from bitter sorrow? 'How about going now?'

Pujol nodded enthusiastically.

'Hop in.'

Pujol awkwardly climbed in and sat. 'Is it far?'

'It won't take more than forty minutes. You'd better do up the seat belt or we'll have the police on our tails.' He smiled and Pujol laughed, though it was clear he did so without understanding. He made no effort to position the seat belt and fasten it and Alvarez had to show him what to do and how to release it.

They had been driving for five minutes when Pujol said: 'Where are we going?'

'Puerto Llueso first of all, then Llueso.'

'Are they beautiful?'

'As beautiful as anywhere in the world.'

'Then we'll find him there.'

'Find who?'

'Frederico. Marta said he's gone to a beautiful place.'

Alvarez knew deep pity and uneasy bewilderment. How was he to make Pujol's disturbed mind understand? 'Who will be in Llueso, Alberto?'

'Frederico.'

'But he can't be because . . .'

'Marta said he would be.'

Alvarez braked the car to a halt. 'Alberto, you must understand that there is always great sadness in the world; more sadness than there is happiness. And to have someone we love die is the most terrible sadness we have to suffer because we can no longer meet and talk. When Marta said that Frederico had gone to a beautiful place, she meant heaven. One day you will find him again, but here on earth you cannot.'

'You must hurry before he leaves.'

Alvarez drove off.

'Quicker. Quicker.'

'Alberto, he is dead. The Frederico you knew left that body when it hit the ground.'

'He . . . he won't be in Llueso?'

'That is impossible.'

Pujol began to cry once more.

They parked by the harbour, enlarged over the years until it moored such a wealth of yachts that it was difficult to remember when it had held only a few fishing boats. Alvarez led the way towards the eastern arm and an ice-cream stall. 'Would you like one?'

Pujol nodded vigorously.

'What flavour is your favourite? Chocolate?'

Pujol stared at the tubs of different flavoured ice-cream set in an ice cabinet. He pointed first at one, then at another, overcome by the choice and only after much havering and a change of one of the flavours at the last moment – to the annoyance of the young girl who was serving – did he decide on a triple cone with chocolate, strawberry, and pistachio.

They walked up the harbour arm, past the fish restaurant and along the recent extension to the outside breakwater, from the top of which they could look across the bay. The water was a vivid blue; with the sun on them, the mountains were majestic, not menacing; a couple of sailing boats ghosted across the water, their multi-coloured sails barely filled; as an added bonus, for once there was not a single power boat underway to destroy the peace. 'There! Isn't that beautiful?'

'Where are the goats?'

Alvarez sighed. 'We'll go in a minute to try and find them.' It had been a waste of time to bring Pujol here in order to appreciate the beauty – perhaps he had done so more for his own pleasure than the other's . . . A brief, choking sound made him turn. Pujol's right arm was hanging by his side so that the half-eaten cone pointed downwards; two of the scoops of ice cream had fallen and were now coloured splotches on the road and the third one was about to follow suit; he was weeping.

Alvarez tried to find words that might bring some comfort, but had spoken no more than a couple when Pujol said in a trembling voice: 'He hit me.'

'Who did?' Alvarez's anger was immediate.

'He . . . he hit me.'

Alvarez put his arm around Pujol's shoulder and led him along to a concrete bench. As he sat, Pujol dropped the cone and kicked it, to send it skittering across the road and over the side into the water by the bows of a large yacht. He leaned forward, buried his face in his hands, and his shoulders shook. A couple walking past stared curiously until Alvarez returned their gaze with such anger at their curiosity that they hurriedly looked away and quickened their rate of walking. 'Who hit you?'

Pujol continued to weep.

Those who lived in the valley held ancient, almost primitive values. Whilst there had been Ferrer, and many others, to offer affection, there had been one who feared the unusual; for him, fear had been so great that he had lost all sense of compassion. But to understand this was not, and never could be, to condone it. On his return to the village, he would face the assailant and persuade him, with threats if need be, never to strike Pujol again. 'Alberto, you must tell me – who hit you?'

Pujol raised his head to say, 'Frederico,' then pressed it down in his hands once more.

The other's mind had become even more divorced from reality than usual, unhinged by sorrow. So had he been hit by anyone or was that nonsense? 'When did someone hit you?'

'The other day.' His words were muffled and, because of his slight speech impediment, even more difficult to understand than usual.

'Can you say exactly which day?'

'You were there.'

Final confirmation that it was arrant nonsense. But then Alvarez realized that he was mistakenly assuming that because Pujol said one thing that was ridiculous, everything else he said had to be equally so. 'Do you mean you were hit the day you saw me near the fountain?'

Pujol nodded.

'Who hit you on that day?'

'Frederico.'

'But he loved you as a son. He could never have struck you.'

177

'He hit me.'

'Why should he ever have done such a thing?'

'It was just getting light. The goats stay together when it's dark and it's easier to count them when they're together. I saw a genet last week. Have you ever seen a genet?'

'Not for many years.'

'Do you know how to make a trap to catch them?'

'Tell me why you keep saying . . .'

'With twigs and string. It's easy.'

'Will you show me how?'

Pujol excitedly nodded.

'Did anyone really hit you the day Frederico died?'

'He hit me.'

'Why?'

'I get up early to see the most goats.'

'You were going to look for goats?'

'I said I'd go with him and show him.'

'And you did?'

'He wouldn't let me. So I followed him. And when he saw me, he hit me to make me go away.' He began to cry once more.

After a while, he ceased crying and began to mutter to himself. Alvarez gained his attention by suggesting they leave and drive into the Parelona peninsula because one often saw wild goats among the mountains and hills which ran the length of that.

They were abreast of a top-heavy, gin-palace of a motor yacht when Alvarez said: 'Tell me, did someone really hit you?'

Pujol repeated what he'd said before.

It was the repetition without a single salient feature contradicted which finally persuaded Alvarez that he was hearing the truth and not wild imagination, born of frantic grief. Only one thing could have induced Frederico to hit Pujol – the desperate and overwhelming need to be on his own; the only reason for that had to be . . . 'Tell me, Alberto, where were you when

Frederico found you'd been following him and he hit you?'

'Near the fountain.'

CHAPTER 26

Alvarez braked the Ibiza to a stop when level with the first house. Pujol opened the door and walked off, not bothering either to thank him or to shut the door. He had taken no more than half a dozen steps when the small white dog with a curly tail appeared and excitedly rushed up. He picked it up and, cradling it in his arms, continued on and out of sight.

Alvarez pulled the passenger door shut, but did not immediately drive off. He stared through the windscreen at the valley. A second Garden of Eden in which the serpent had lured Beatriz Ruig into eating the fruit of the tree of the knowledge of good and evil . . .

It had taken him long enough to learn the truth because he was a peasant without the wit to understand that if something was impossible, it was not possible. Yet though a clever man, Garicano would never learn the truth because he was not a peasant.

Garicano would – since he'd never willingly admit failure – come to the conclusion that there could not – as he had already suggested – be any connection between the two deaths. As Beatriz Ruig had died when on her own and there was no known motive for Ferrer's murder, his death had been accidental. And the movement of his corpse was easily explained – one of the villagers rolled it over when stupidly searching for signs of life in spite of the horrific injuries and, being all but a moron, had never reported that fact.

Garicano would fail to uncover the truth because he was psychologically incapable of understanding the minds of those who lived in the valley. Try to explain that for them the fountain was so much more than a column of water; recall the fact that when the fountain had suddenly appeared the villagers had acclaimed it a miracle and that their belief had redoubled when the church had tried to deny them it; suggest that this belief had gained such strength and mystical significance that it had become religious in nature and survived into an age when beyond the valley there was near universal disbelief; talk about the need to placate by sacrifice . . . And he would scornfully, contemptuously express his inability to understand such arrant stupidity.

In a valley where there was no television and probably no radio, where the outside world meant little more than people who came and looked at the fountain and the workers with the same witless curiosity, everything that happened was of the utmost interest to them all. Either Amelia or Lucía had overheard Tait's bargaining with Beatriz Ruig. This had alerted everyone to the fact that the whole inner meaning of their lives was threatened. If the valley were sold and they were thrown out because they were only share-croppers, they would never again be able to worship 'their' fountain. Frederico had pleaded with her not to sell. But however impassioned his plea, it could never alter her decision because her god was money, not a fountain.

Again through Amelia or Lucía, they had known the sale was almost completed. So when Tait had driven up to the house that Thursday evening, they had come to the conclusion, both true and false, that he was about to close the deal. After he'd left the valley, Frederico, probably with one or two others, had gone up to the house to make one last, desperate appeal to her. She had told them that the valley would very soon be sold and they would have to leave. Mallorquins were descended from a rich stew of races – Phoenicians, Greeks, Romans, Arabs, Catalans – and it was perhaps this mixture which was largely responsible for their occasional, explosive surges of emotion.

Frederico's emotions had overwhelmed him and instead of the mild man who quietly suffered all the slings and arrows of outrageous fortune thrown at him, he had suddenly become wild-eyed, prophesying her eternal damnation if she went ahead with the sale. In his frenzy, he had appeared capable of anything and when he had touched her, probably inadvertently, certainly not with the intention of actually hurting her, she had been so terrified that she had suffered vagal inhibition and died, hitting her head on something in the study as she fell.

Her death had instantly restored Frederico to his senses. He had found himself with a dead woman at his feet. Who would believe he had not murdered her? Perhaps his companions even believed he had, through spiritual forces.

A peasant, however slow of speech, however limited his knowledge of the wider world, was not necessarily stupid. Frederico had judged that his only way of avoiding a charge of murder was to make it appear she had died a natural death when on her own. He had called on the villagers to help him.

It had not occurred even to him to retrieve the mobile phone; he had been unable to appreciate that its presence in the study could hold a significance. So they had left it there when they'd carried her body up to the bedroom. The men had left, the women had undressed the corpse and then dressed it, because of the need to honour it, in the nightdress that was part of her never-used trousseau. (Alvarez remembered how he had assumed she had slept in finery because of a hopeless yearning for a missed happiness. Why had he not asked himself the question, if that were so, how was the nightdress in pristine condition after so many years of frustration?) They had worked by candlelight. Having always watched every peseta, the last to leave the room had naturally blown out the candle . . .

The next morning, the women had returned and locked and bolted themselves inside the room. The men had smashed the door down. The scene had been set to make

182

it obvious that the señorita must have been on her own when she died . . .

Garicano had come to that conclusion because he was smart and therefore unable to appreciate that stupidity could be slyly clever. Contemptuously, he had never considered the possibility that they might all have been lying. As Carlos Almunia had written, 'It is easier to make a fool of a wise man than a simpleton.'

But, of course, it was impossible to turn a simpleton into a wise man. He – Alvarez – had been called to the case merely to confirm. With witless incompetence, he had set out to contradict. And whilst a snuffed-out candle and a forgotten mobile phone had alerted him to the truth, he had then hidden that truth from himself by attempting to discover how the impossible could be possible. Even a man of moderate intelligence knew that it could not be . . .

Frederico had made a point of being friendly and so to some extent had learned how the investigation was proceeding. But without sufficient information to judge accurately, it had seemed to him that not only was he – Alvarez – convinced the señorita had not been on her own, but that he was making far more progress in uncovering the truth than, in fact, he was. Amelia must have told Frederico about the attempts to secure the bedroom shutter from the outside and how this had seemingly proved to be impossible. Burdened with the truth, he had been far too ready to believe that this certainty must show that he had been present when she died. That she had died because of him, yet without any wish on his part for her death, was the truth. Yet who in authority would believe him innocent of motive? . . .

Expiation by sacrifice. Many religions had once believed in that. He had decided to commit suicide before the fountain. Before he had succeeded, he had had to bear the additional pain of driving away Pujol. Even in success, he had failed. When the villagers had come to honour his crushed body, they had discovered that he had misjudged the path of his fall and had died beyond the direct line of sight of the fountain. They had moved his body . . .

Alvarez checked the time. Amelia or Lucía might still be working at Son Abrut. He drove slowly to the house, knowing that for his own satisfaction he must try to discover whether he had finally reached the truth, yet illogically frightened that by doing so he might cause the truth to be broadcast.

He entered the house and called out. Seconds later, Amelia stepped out of the study. He said: 'I don't see Inspector Garicano's car so I suppose he's gone?'

'Went off in a rush some time ago.'

'As energetic as ever. Makes a man tired just to watch him . . . Can you give me a hand for a moment?'

'Don't see why not. Nearly finished anyway. What's up?'

'There's one more thing to check quickly before I'm finished with the case. So if we go upstairs . . .' He led the way up to the sala and Beatriz Ruig's bedroom. After opening the shutters, he crossed to the cumbersome chest of drawers. 'If I hand you the clothes, will you put them on the bed?'

'What clothes?'

'The ones in the two bottom drawers.'

'What d'you want with them?'

He didn't answer her, opened the second drawer from the bottom and lifted out a garment wrapped in green tissue paper. After undoing the paper, he examined a pair of embroidered silk knickers whose voluminous pattern would have made a modern young lady laugh scornfully. As he passed the knickers to her, she said: 'It ain't right, you looking at 'em like this.'

Like so many peasant women, she was both broad-minded and extraordinarily prudish and now she was embarrassed by his actions. He lifted out a second pair of knickers, identical in pattern but with a different embroidery. 'A detective sometimes has to be like a doctor and concern himself with intimate matters.'

184

'And there's doctors too fond of doing that!'

He slowly emptied the drawer, started on the second one which contained larger garments. In turn, he handed her petticoats and nightdresses, all made from the finest quality silk. He indicated the embroidery around the neck of the third nightdress. 'It's some of the finest work I've ever seen.'

'They say she did it all, but I've never seen her with a needle.'

'Must be a tricky job to wash and iron anything this fine. I suppose to get out all the creases you need a really hot iron . . .'

'On silk? That'd ruin it in half a second. Maybe you know more about your job than you do about ironing?'

'So how d'you go about things, then?'

'Use a moderate iron on the wrong side when the silk's damp.'

'Not so easy to judge without electricity and so no thermostat.'

'D'you think no one could iron fifty years back? You spit and watch how much the spit jumps around.'

'So I guess you have to do a lot of spitting when you're ironing this stuff?'

'Never ironed any of it.'

'How's that?'

'Can't you understand that it's her trousseau?'

'Yes, I know, but I was reckoning that when she realized she wasn't ever going to marry, she'd start wearing things to get some use from them.'

'You men!' she said, with a scorn that Dolores would have admired. 'No one ever told you it's terrible luck to wear anything from a trousseau before getting married? With her being so superstitious, she wouldn't have touched any of this, not even if she'd been freezing to death.'

'Yet she was wearing a fourth nightdress in the morning . . . I suppose it was even more important that outsiders saw her in finery and not rags than it was that in death she risked the perils of an ancient superstition?'

She was shocked to discover that she had allowed herself to be trapped into betraying the truth. Instinctively, she sought the ancient defence of all peasants. She stared at the floor, a bovine expression of vacuity on her face.

'Is something wrong?' Dolores asked.

Alvarez hurriedly spoke through a mouthful of Panada de carn i carxofes. 'Nothing. It's absolutely delicious.'

'I'm not talking about the food.'

He was no less surprised than Jaime or the children.

'You've looked sad and unhappy since you arrived home. Have you been seeing . . .' She did not finish. She silently cursed all foreign putas who stole the wits of decent, if weak, Mallorquin men.

'I am sad and unhappy,' he finally admitted.

'Because of her?'

'Because it distresses me to learn how easily a smile can conceal a black heart.'

'What are you on about?' Jaime demanded.

'I've been investigating three Englishmen. Meet any of 'em casually and you'd think he was just an ordinary, decent person – for a foreigner, that is. Yet each of them has a dark secret. So the question has to be, how many other men's smiles conceal black truths?'

'All,' snapped Dolores.

CHAPTER 27

'Before she went out,' Lavinia said, 'Diana insisted on having a talk with me.'

'What about?' Grenville-Varney sat within the shade of the large sun umbrella.

'That man. She intends to marry him, whatever we say.'

'Can't understand the modern generation. No sense of duty.' He turned and looked at his wife as he added, with some surprise: 'I must say, old girl, you don't sound all that shocked by the mésalliance!'

'She told me something more. He's inherited quite a lot of land from his aunt.'

'The one he murdered?'

'I don't think he can have done or surely he'd be under arrest?'

'In this country, they still wouldn't have got around to arresting Crippen . . . She's intending to marry a farmer! Good God!'

'Apparently he's selling the land. To some Japanese.'

'Sounds unlikely. What would little yellow men want with land on this island?'

'They intend to build a golf course.'

'Didn't know they'd advanced beyond chopping each other to bits with samurai swords.' He lifted the bottle of Heidsieck out of the silver ice bucket, stretched across the table to refill her glass. 'I take it you've told her that if she does marry him, she can't expect an allowance?'

'Of course.'

'She's not cut out to live in poverty, so she'll soon come to her senses.'

'I don't think she'll have to. The Japanese are paying just under a million and a half dollars for the land.'

'They're *what*?'

'I know! And apparently they would have paid two million if that funny little man hadn't persuaded Mason . . .'

'What funny little man?'

'The detective who came here and made a nuisance of himself. He persuaded Mason to say that the peasants must be allowed to stay in their shacks if they want to. That naturally reduced the price. I mean, who'd want to play golf with that sort of person in sight? What's more, Mason said they had to have access to the fountain and have the right to some of the water which seems to be very important to them.'

'Can't be. None of 'em wash.'

'Diana wanted to explain what it was all about, but I really couldn't be bothered to listen.'

He finally refilled his own glass, replaced the bottle in the ice bucket. He drank. He stared at the rising bubbles in the flute. 'Thrown away half a million dollars because of a few peasants? The man's not just a ranker, he's . . . Good God, he's also a damned socialist.'

DATE		